"We made a b

Her eyes widened s
topic?"

"Not for much long

"I know, but we have a plan, right? Pretend dating."

Pretend dating meant putting on a show—mostly for *his* family. And not getting involved in any way. They could be friends, but nothing more.

Friends who sleep together, he thought hopefully, and then reminded himself he'd sworn off women again. He had to. Look at what had happened with Rachel.

Women were the root of all the trouble in his life and he would be better off if he could simply walk away from them.

Then Rachel smiled and he found himself wanting her again.

Walking away wasn't an option.

Dear Reader,

I hope you're having as much fun reading the
POSITIVELY PREGNANT series as I had writing it.
One of the things I love most about these books is that
much of what happens to the characters is unexpected.

Have you ever met someone and later found out there
were so many things you didn't know about that person?
So many good things that made you like him or her even
more? That's a concept I'm having fun with in this series.
Unexpected people, unexpected relationships, unexpected
babies! Falling in love is always a gift, but falling in love
with someone unexpected is even more fun.

Rachel Harper thinks she's someone who enjoys surprises,
but she has kind of gotten into a rut. Carter Brockett is
just the man to nudge her into love's fast lane, but what
happens when the ride takes off in a direction neither of
them expected?

I hope you enjoy *The Ladies' Man*.

Best,

Susan Mallery

SUSAN MALLERY

THE LADIES' MAN

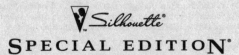

SPECIAL EDITION®

Published by Silhouette Books

America's Publisher of Contemporary Romance

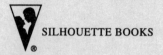 **SILHOUETTE BOOKS**

ISBN-13: 978-0-373-24778-3
ISBN-10:   0-373-24778-8

THE LADIES' MAN

Copyright © 2006 by Susan Macias Redmond

Visit Silhouette Books at www.eHarlequin.com

Printed in U.S.A.

SUSAN MALLERY

is the bestselling and award-winning author of over fifty books for Harlequin and Silhouette Books. She makes her home in the Los Angeles area with her handsome prince of a husband, her two adorable-but-not-bright cats and new puppy. Check out all her doings at www.susanmallery.com.

Chapter One

Rachel Harper had always longed to be more sophisticated. It was right there on her to-do list between "be more aware of current events" and "don't let your handwashing pile up so much."

While she *had* started watching the national news nearly every night, she wasn't doing so well keeping up with her delicates. And the sophistication thing? A total loss.

Which was why she found herself, at the ripe old age of twenty-five, sitting in a bar and feeling as if she didn't have a clue as to how to act. Not that she was here to do normal barlike things. Instead, she'd agreed to accompany Diane, a new teacher at her school, who was breaking up with her boyfriend and had asked Rachel to come along for moral support. As the next item of Rachel's to-do list—right under the issue with the hand-washing—was "get out more," she'd agreed to tag along to the Blue Dog Bar.

Rachel wasn't sure what dog, blue or not, had inspired the name. There seemed to be a lot more men than women in the bar. She swirled the margarita she'd ordered, then took a big sip.

"The jerk isn't even going to show up," Diane said from her seat across the small table they'd chosen by the wall. "That is so like him. I swear, I'm going to kick him in the head when I see him." Diane paused, then smiled. "See, I'm talking in 'I' sentences, just like that book said."

"Yes, you are," Rachel murmured, deciding not to point out that the "I" sentences the self-help manual referred to probably didn't fall into the "I'm going to kick you in the head" category.

"There he is," Diane said as she stood. "Wish me luck."

Rachel glanced at the tall, dark-haired man who strolled into the bar, looking as if he could take just about every other guy there. "Good luck," she said and meant it.

Carter Brockett eyed the curvy brunette in the prim dress and knew he was seconds away from all kinds of trouble. The cool, logical side of his brain reminded him that all the pain and suffering in his life could be traced back to one source: women. Life was always better when he walked away.

The part of his brain—and the rest of him—that enjoyed a warm body, a sharp mind and a purely feminine take on the world said she looked interesting. And that last bit of consciousness, shaped by a very strong-willed mother who had drilled into him that he was always to protect those weaker than him, told him that the attractive brunette was in way over her head.

He could be wrong of course. For all he knew, she was a leather-wearing dominatrix who came to the Blue Dog because of the place's reputation. But he had his doubts.

The Blue Dog was a cop bar. But not just any hangout for those in uniform. It was a place where guys showed up to get lucky and the women who walked in counted on that fact. Carter usually avoided the place—he worked undercover and couldn't afford to be seen here. But one of his contacts had insisted on the location, so Carter had agreed and prayed no one from the force would speak to him.

No one had. He'd concluded his business and had been about to leave when the brunette had walked in with her friend, who was currently involved in a heated conversation with Eddy. Eddy wasn't exactly a prince when it came to his dating habits, so Carter had a feeling the chat wasn't going to go well. He nodded at Jenny, the bartender on duty, then pointed to the brunette. Jenny raised her eyebrows.

Carter didn't have to guess what she was thinking. Jenny, an ex-girlfriend, knew him pretty well. Yeah, well, maybe after a few months of self-induced celibacy, he was ready to give the man-woman thing another try. Even though he knew better. Even though it was always a disaster.

He glanced around and saw he wasn't the only one who'd noticed the contrast between the brunette's made-for-sin body and her Sunday-school-teacher clothes. So if he was going to protect her from the other big bad cops, he'd better get a move on.

He walked to the bar, where Jenny handed him a beer and a margarita. He ignored her knowing grin and crossed to the brunette's table.

"Hi. I'm Carter. Mind if I join you?"

As he asked the question, he set down the margarita and gave her his best smile.

Yeah, yeah, a cheap trick, he thought, remembering all the hours he'd spent perfecting it back in high school. He'd taught himself to smile with just the right amount of interest, charm and bashfulness. It never failed.

Not even tonight, when the woman looked up, flushed, half rose, then sat back down, and in the process knocked over her nearly empty drink and scattered the slushy contents across the table and down the front of her dress.

"Oh, no," she said, her voice soft and almost musical. "Darn. I can't believe I…" She pressed her lips together, then looked at him.

He'd already sopped up the mess on the table with a couple of napkins. He completely ignored the dampness on her dress. Sure, he was interested, but he wasn't stupid.

"You okay?" he asked, curious about a woman who actually said *darn*.

"Yes. Thank you."

He passed over the drink he'd brought.

She glanced first at it, then at him. "I'm, ah, with someone."

He kept his gaze on her. "Your girlfriend. I saw you come in together."

She nodded. "She's breaking up with her boyfriend and wanted moral support. I don't usually... This isn't..." She sighed. "She'll be back soon."

"No problem," he said easily. "I'll keep you company until she's finished."

Even in the dim light of the bar, he could see her eyes were green. Her long, dark hair hung in sensuous waves to just past her shoulders.

Carter held in a snort. Sensuous waves? He'd sure been without for a little too long if he were thinking things like that.

She shifted uncomfortably and didn't touch the drink.

"Is it me or the bar?" he asked.

"What? Oh, both, I suppose." Instantly, she covered her mouth, then dropped her hand to her damp lap. "Sorry. I shouldn't have said that."

"It's fine. I'm a great believer in the truth. So which is more scary?"

She glanced around the Blue Dog, then returned her attention to him. "Mostly you."

He grinned. "I'm flattered."

"Why? You *want* me to think you're scary?"

He leaned forward and lowered his voice just enough to get her to sway toward him. "Not scary. Dangerous. All guys want to be dangerous. Women love that."

She surprised him by laughing. "Okay, Carter, I can see you're a pro and I'm way out of my league with you. I cheerfully confess I'm not the bar type and being in this setting makes me horribly uncomfortable." She glanced at her friend. "I can't tell if the fight's going well or badly. What do you think?"

He looked at Eddy, who'd backed the blonde into a corner. "It depends on how you're defining 'well.' I don't think they're actually breaking up. Do you?"

"I'm not sure. Diane was determined to tell him what she thought, once and for all. In 'I' sentences."

He frowned. "In what?"

She smiled. "*I* think you're not treating me with respect. *I* think you're always late on purpose. That kind of thing. Although she did say something about wanting to kick him in the head, which is unlikely to help. Of course, I don't know Eddy. He may like that sort of thing."

Carter was totally and completely charmed. "Who *are* you?" he asked.

"My name is Rachel."

"You don't swear, you don't hang out in bars, so what do you do?"

"How do you know I don't swear?" she asked.

"You said 'darn' when you spilled your drink."

"Oh. Right. It's a habit. I teach kindergarten. There's no way I can swear in front of the children, not that I ever used a lot of bad words, so I trained myself to never say them. It's just easier. So I use words like 'darn' and 'golly.'" She grinned. "Sometimes people look at me like I'm at the dull-normal end of the IQ scale, but I can live with that. It's for the greater good. So who are you?"

A complicated question, Carter thought, knowing he couldn't tell her the truth. "Just a guy."

"Uh-huh." She eyed his earring—a diamond stud—and his too-long hair. "More than just a guy. What do you do?"

That changed with the assignment, he thought. "I'm working for a chopper shop. Motorcycles," he added.

She straightened her spine and squared her shoulders. "I know what a chopper is. I'm not some innocent fresh out of the backwoods."

Her indignation made him want to chuckle. She reminded him of a kitten facing down a very large and powerful dog. All the arched back and hissing fury didn't make the kitten any bigger.

"Not a lot of backwoods around here," he said easily. "Desert, though. You could be an innocent fresh out of the desert."

Her lips twitched, as if she were trying not to smile. He pushed her margarita toward her.

"You're letting all the ice melt," he told her.

She hesitated, then took a sip. "Are you from around here?" she asked.

"Born and raised. All my family's here."

"Such as?"

Now it was his turn to pause. He didn't usually give out personal information. In his line of work, it could get him into trouble. But he had a feeling Rachel wasn't going to be a threat to much more than his oath of celibacy.

"Three sisters, a mom. Their main purpose in life is

to make me crazy." He made the statement with equal parts love and exasperation.

Rachel looked wistful. "That's nice. Not the crazy part, but that you're close."

"You're not close to your family?"

"I don't have any."

He didn't know what to say to that and reminded himself too late that he was supposed to be charming her, not reminding her that she was alone in the world.

"Are you from around here?" he asked.

"Riverside?" She shook her head. Her hair swayed and caught the light and, for the moment, totally mesmerized him. "I moved here after I graduated from college. I wanted a nice, quiet, suburban sort of place." She sighed. "Not very exciting."

"Hey, I've lived here all my life. I can show you the best spots for viewing the submarine races."

She grinned. "Where I grew up, we went parking over by the river. Well, not really a river. More of a gully. Part of the year, it even had water in it."

"Parking, huh?"

She shrugged. "I had my moments."

"And now?"

Her gaze drifted to where her friend still talked to Eddy. "Not so much." She looked back at him. "Why'd you come over?"

He smiled. "Have you looked in the mirror lately?"

She ducked her head and blushed. Carter couldn't remember the last time he'd seen a woman blush. He wanted to make her do it again.

"Thank you," she said. "I spend my days with five-year-olds whose idea of being charming is to put glue in my hair. You're a nice change."

"You're comparing me to a five-year-old?" he asked, pretending outrage.

"Well, a lot of guys have maturity issues."

"I'm totally mature. Responsible, even."

She didn't look convinced. "Of course you are."

Carter was…interesting, Rachel thought, then nearly laughed out loud at the wild understatement. Okay, he was gorgeous, in a California blond, male-model sort of way. Classically handsome with shaggy hair and that earring. Who had given it to him? She couldn't stop looking at it, which told her she needed to get out more. No wait—that was already on her to-do list.

He was big, with broad shoulders and a smile that made her toes curl inside her sensible, low-heeled pumps even as she wondered if there were any interesting tattoos underneath the chambray shirt and jeans. What would it be like to be a leather-and-lace kind of woman—someone who knew what to do with a guy like Carter? As it was she was blushing, practically stammering and wishing Diane would hurry up so they could go.

Except she wasn't ready to leave. Not just yet. Carter wasn't the kind of guy who usually came on to her, but it was fun to play "what-if" even if only in her head.

So she took a drink of her margarita and imagined herself to be wearing a wicked red-lace bra and a matching thong under black leather and some low-cut bustier. What would *that* Rachel say to a man like him?

"So tell me a secret," she said, surprising herself and, from the way his eyebrows lifted, him.

Her instinct was to take it back and say he didn't have to, but she refused to crumble now.

He thought for a second, then shrugged. "I keep trying to give up on women. They invade every part of my life and I know I'd be better off if I could just stay away from them. I was raised to do the right thing, so once I'm involved it's hard to get out."

Not the answer she'd expected. "You know I'm a woman, right?" she asked, only half kidding.

He grinned. "Oh, yeah. I noticed."

"You're going to give up women by not avoiding them?"

He sipped his beer. "It's a work in progress," he admitted. "I avoid them for a few months and then I walk into somewhere safe and I'm sucker punched by someone I didn't expect."

Did that mean her?

"So tell me your secret," he said.

"I dance," she admitted without thinking, then immediately wished she could call back the words. "I mean, I used to. When I was growing up and in college. I wanted to be a dancer, but I don't have the right body type."

He was polite enough to keep his gaze firmly fixed on her face.

"What kind of dance?" he asked.

"Everything. Ballet, jazz, modern. I still take classes, which is silly because it's not like I'm going to do something with it."

"Why is it silly? Does everything have to have a purpose?"

She didn't know how to answer. She'd never told anyone about her dancing and she wasn't sure why she'd admitted it now. Maybe because it was easier than talking about her leather-and-lace fantasy.

Before she could answer his question, Diane's sharp voice cut across the floor.

"You're a jerk, Eddy. I don't know why I ever bothered with you."

"Hey, babe, don't be that way."

Eddy reached for Diane, who pushed his arm away. "I hate you. How's that for an *I* sentence. Go to hell."

Eddy threw up both hands. "I don't need this from you. Just forget it."

Diane glared at him. "Fine, I will. This is the end. Don't bother coming around again. Understand."

"Clearly. Don't you come crawling back. I'm not interested."

"Me, either."

With that, Diane whirled around and marched out of the bar.

Rachel stared after her. "She said she wanted to break up with him, but I didn't think she meant it." She looked at the exit, wondering if her friend would be all right. "I need to go check on her."

"Sure thing."

Rachel stood, as did Carter. She glanced from him to the door and back.

"Thanks for the drink and the conversation," she said, suddenly feeling awkward. "You were really nice."

His easy smile gave her toes another miniworkout. "Words every guy longs to hear."

"What? Oh." She laughed. "Right. Sorry. You were especially dangerous tonight. I was terrified."

"Better."

He stepped around the table and lightly kissed her. She had no warning. One second he was moving and the next she felt a soft, tempting pressure on her mouth that was gone before she could fully grasp it.

"Take care, Rachel," he said and headed back to the bar.

She watched him go, then turned and walked out into the still warm evening. Who could have known she could meet such a great guy in a bar? She glanced at the sign showing a sitting, tail-wagging, blue dog in bright neon. And here, of all places.

At least she could check "get out more" off her to-do list, she thought as she moved toward Diane's car. That was—

The car was gone.

Rachel distinctly remembered where her friend had parked because the ghostly blue from the sign had turned her dress purple as she'd climbed out of the car. As Diane wasn't standing around in hysterics, it was unlikely the car had been stolen.

"But she was my ride home," Rachel said aloud to no one.

Diane had left her? Was that possible? Sure, her friend had been upset, but...

Rachel walked to the edge of the parking lot and glanced up and down the street. Nothing. No familiar blue sedan cruised in her direction.

Her mouth opened and closed. This could not be happening. Sure she didn't know Diane all that well, but how flaky would the other woman have to be to go off and forget her?

"Is there a problem?"

The familiar voice made her want to groan, and not in a good way. She'd been so happy with how things had gone in the bar. She'd managed to act sophisticated and bar-worldly...sort of. But to have all that blown now was really unfair.

She turned until she faced Carter, then shrugged.

"So your girlfriend was more upset than either of us realized," he said, obviously grasping what had happened.

"Apparently."

"Come on," he said with a smile. "I'll take you home."

She wanted to tell him that wasn't necessary. That she would call another friend or a cab. But it was late and she hated to disturb anyone because of what had happened, and this was Riverside, not New York. There weren't exactly cabs cruising around looking for fares.

He held up both hands, as if surrendering. "I'm perfectly safe."

"Ha. You said you were dangerous."

"Only in my dreams."

He tilted his head in invitation. She sighed, then nodded.

"Thank you," she said as she followed him to a large black truck.

"No problem. This can be my good deed for the week. It'll make my mom happy."

Him mentioning his mother eased a little of her tension. She felt awkward as she climbed onto the passenger seat, which felt about thirty feet above the ground.

"Nice truck," she said when he slid in on the driver's side. "Great visibility."

"Macho," he corrected with a grin. "Macho truck."

She couldn't help laughing. "Of course. My mistake. Imagine how high it would be if you got those really big tires."

"Not my style."

Oh, but a truck was? And people said women were confusing.

He started the engine, then glanced at her. "Where to?"

She fastened her seat belt and gave him directions.

After Carter pulled out of the parking lot, he said, "You need to have a talk with your friend. Driving off and leaving you alone at a bar is not okay."

"I agree. I couldn't believe it when I stepped out and her car was gone. I don't know her all that well, but still…" She shrugged.

"You work together?" he asked.

"Yes. She just started this term. Diane teaches fourth grade."

"Big kids," he teased.

"Bigger than mine. Plus I suspect by the time they're nine there's a whole lot less paste eating. But I wouldn't trade. I love the little kids. Everything is exciting and new to them. They see all the possibilities. If I do my job right, I can help them love school for the rest of their lives."

Just then his cell phone rang. He pulled it out of his shirt pocket and flipped it open.

"Brockett. Uh-huh. Yeah. How'd you know?" He laughed. "No. I've got it. Night." He hung up. "Your friend came back, looking for you."

"Really? Good. I didn't want to have to yell at her tomorrow. Who called?"

"Jenny, the bartender. She'll tell Diane that you're good."

Rachel opened her mouth, then closed it. She wasn't sure "good" covered it. There was every possibility that Diane would think she was going home with a guy she just met. Perhaps not the most awful thing in the world, but not a reality Rachel was comfortable with.

As she couldn't discuss that with Carter, she asked the next logical question.

"How does the bartender know your cell number?"

"Don't panic," he told her. "I'm not that much of a regular. Jenny and I go way back. We've been friends for years."

Friends, huh? And before that?

He pulled up in front of her small apartment building. It was in an older part of town. Rachel had chosen the place specifically because she loved the higher ceilings

and custom touches of the Craftsman-style archi-
tecture.

Carter turned off the engine, then looked at the
carport. "Let me guess," he said, eyeing the cars parked
there. "The gray sedan."

She unfastened her seat belt and had the satisfaction
of knowing she was about to shock him. "The little red,
two-seater convertible."

His eyes widened. "No way."

"Way."

His gaze settled on her face. "Why wasn't my kindergarten teacher more like you?"

"Maybe she was. Five-year-olds tend not to notice
stuff like that."

"I guess."

Before she could thank him for the ride, he climbed
out of the truck. She did the same and they met on the
sidewalk.

"You don't have to walk me up," she said.

"I want to. This is a full-service rescue."

She felt nervous and out of her element, but not
afraid. She liked Carter and while she knew she would
probably never see him again, she couldn't help being
glad he didn't want to run right off.

She led the way up the stairs to the far apartment. As
they passed between her overflowing plant stands, he
asked, "Yours?"

She pulled her keys out of her purse. "Another hobby.
I like to grow things."

"A kindergarten teacher who dances and has a green

thumb. Interesting." He stepped a little closer and lightly touched her cheek with his fingertips. "I'm going to kiss you, Rachel. I'm telling you this in advance, so you can race inside, slap me or go with it and kiss me back. We all know what my choice would be, but you get a say in this, too."

The porch light brought out the gold in his blond hair. He was both handsome and sexy, a fairly irresistible combination. She hadn't been on a date in months or been kissed in nearly two years and until this exact moment, hadn't realized how much she'd missed having a man in her life.

"I'm not the slapping type," she murmured, her gaze locked with his.

He gave her a slow, knowing smile that made her shiver.

"Good to know," he said, right before he kissed her.

Chapter Two

Carter's mouth was warm and firm on hers, but tender. Rachel had thought he might be one of those pushy kissers, claiming what he wanted. Instead he moved back and forth against her mouth, giving just enough to make her want more.

One of them moved toward the other. She wasn't sure who was responsible for the sudden closeness, but she wasn't going to complain about the feel of his hard, muscled body pressing against hers. He smelled good—like the outdoors, with a hint of masculine temptation. Heat radiated from him, making her want to cuddle even closer, like a cat looking for a sunny spot.

One of his hands continued to stroke her cheek, lightly brushing against her skin, while the other rested on her waist. She wondered if he were holding her in place. Had her mouth not been so busy pressing up against his, she would have told him that she had no intention of going anywhere.

He brushed the very tip of his tongue against her lower lip. The tiny movement was both exciting and erotic. She parted for him, then held her breath in anticipation of him deepening the kiss.

He moved forward slowly, cautiously, as if giving her time to retreat. Instead all she could think was how long it had been since she'd really kissed a man. Not since she'd broken off her engagement nearly two years ago.

At the exact moment his tongue gently stroked hers, need exploded inside of her. The intensity was as shocking as it was unexpected. She wanted more, needed more. Her body suddenly ached to have him touching her. Skin tightened, her breasts swelled. She let her purse slip to the ground, then wrapped both arms around his neck and leaned into him.

He accepted her with a low groan that made her nipples tighten. He pulled her against him, even as he ran his hands up and down her back. She tilted her head and he deepened the kiss, exploring all of her mouth with an urgency that made her tremble.

The depth of passion stunned her. She'd never felt like this from just a kiss and certainly never with a man she'd just met. It was insane. It was also thrilling and arousing and so not anything she was used to.

Carter pulled back slightly. He kissed her cheeks, then along her jaw and down her neck.

"You're so beautiful," he murmured. "Are you trying to make guys crazy on purpose?"

She could barely breathe, let alone speak, but she forced herself to gather her thoughts. "What are you talking about?"

"Those damn curves in that prim little dress," he muttered as he licked the sensitive skin just below her ear. "It shouldn't be legal."

Her eyes popped open and she stared into the darkness of the night. "Me?" she asked in a voice that squeaked. "But I need to lose about fifteen pounds." Twenty, really, but she couldn't bring herself to say that aloud. "I'm not…"

"Incredible?" he asked, brushing her mouth with his. "Sexy? Stunning?" He straightened and smiled. "If this wasn't the first time I'd kissed you and if I hadn't been raised to know better, I'd show you exactly what you've done to me."

Curiosity exploded. Was he talking about what she thought he was talking about? Had she really aroused him?

For her own part, she felt more than a little tingly, but he was so much more cool than she could ever hope to be.

She looked into his dark eyes and saw fire burning there. His desire matched her own growing need.

"I've never…" she said, then cleared her throat. "I don't…"

"I know," he said with more than a little regret. "I swore off sex on the first date about the time I turned twenty. You're not the type." He smiled ruefully. "I'll tell you what, Rachel. You're enough to make me rethink my plan of swearing off women."

He kissed her again, then bent down and picked up her purse. She took it from him and held it in both hands. It was that or reach for him again.

He drew in a deep breath. "Here's what I think. You're gonna go inside your place, smile, thank me for a great evening and close the door." He frowned. "You need to lock it, too."

That made her smile. "You're not the type to break in."

"I don't know. I haven't been this tempted before."

His words made her tremble. She knew his advice was sound, but it was amazingly difficult to force herself to open her door, then step inside alone. Still, she did it. She set her keys and her purse on the small table by the door, then drew in a breath and prepared to tell him goodbye.

She was in his arms. She wasn't sure who made the move, but it didn't matter because holding him and being held felt so good. Even as his mouth claimed hers in a kiss that stirred her to her soul, she savored the feel of his hands as he ran them up and down her back. She could feel the pressure of his fingers, the heat of him. When he lingered on her hips, she instinctively arched toward him. Her belly brushed against his erection.

Need rushed through her. He hadn't been kidding—he *did* want her. Just as she wanted him. Nothing about this made any sense at all, but where men were concerned, she'd always been cautious. She'd had exactly two lovers in her life and she'd waited until she'd been sure they were in love and talking about getting married before giving in. She'd never been with a stranger. Until tonight she'd never even kissed a stranger. She was sure that in the bright light of day she would have given herself a stern talking-to, but right now she didn't care.

She placed her hands on his chest and allowed herself to explore him. As their tongues circled and danced and mated, she learned how she liked to breathe in the scent of his skin.

He set his hands on her waist and moved them up. Slowly, slowly, as if giving her time to protest. Without thinking, she covered his hands with hers and brought them to her breasts.

She was jolted both by her own actions, something she'd never done before, and the exquisite pleasure of having him touch her there. She decided to deal with her guilt later and simply enjoy the feel of him caressing her curves, brushing against her nipples and making her body melt.

The ever-present need grew. She was already wet and swollen and she wanted to be touched everywhere. She squirmed to get closer even as he started unbuttoning the front of her dress.

Yes, she thought hazily. Without clothes they could touch each other. She tugged at his T-shirt. He stepped back, unfastened the buttons and ripped it off. Passion darkened his eyes to the color of the night sky. There was light from a single small lamp in the corner but it was enough to let her see how hard he was breathing and how his desire pushed at the zipper of his jeans.

They came together again. Now she could touch his back and chest, feeling the warmth and smoothness of his skin. He managed to unfasten the front buttons on her dress and push the fabric aside. Her arms were caught for a moment, then she freed herself and shoved it out of the way. Her dress fell to the floor and pooled at her feet.

Under any other circumstances, she would have been embarrassed, but there was no time. Carter bent down and, through her bra, took her nipple in his mouth. She lost herself in the wet heat and gentle sucking. She touched his head, his back, his arms and wished there was a way to touch all of him.

He nudged her backward. She went willingly, then let herself fall onto the sofa. He eased on top of her until they were a tangle of arms and legs. His arousal pressed between her thighs and, even with multiple layers of clothing, he managed to excite that one sensitive spot.

More, she thought frantically, knowing it had been so long and that she would be close in a matter of seconds. She needed more.

He unfastened her bra and pulled it away. Now she felt his mouth on her bare skin and it was nearly enough to send her over the edge. He slipped one hand between them and even as his tongue teased her aching nipple and brought her close to the edge, he eased between her legs and under her panties to get lost in paradise.

He found her center immediately. She didn't know if it was good luck or a lot of practice, and at that moment, she didn't care. He rubbed around the swollen spot before brushing over it. She gasped as her body tightened and every cell waited breathlessly for that one moment of release.

Again and again he touched her, moving steadily, then slower, then faster, pushing her into madness until she could only wait, unable to breathe until her body gave in to the pure pleasure and convulsed into release.

She clung to him as the waves rippled through her. He continued to touch her and she continued to climax until he swore, pulled back, unfastened his jeans, jerked down her panties and plunged inside of her.

He was thick and he filled her until she had no choice but to climax again. They held on to each other, kissing, straining, reaching. He called out her name, then stiffened as his body found its own release, and then they were still.

Rachel savored the weight of him, unable to believe that she, of all people, had really made love with a stranger, on her slip-covered sofa, with the scent of night-blooming jasmine in the air.

Rachel woke a few minutes before her alarm clock went off, to find the sun streaming into the room. That didn't make sense, she thought in sleepy confusion. She always closed the blinds and then pulled the pale curtains. But this morning the curtains were all that were between her and an east-facing window. Huh. Shouldn't she have…

Reality crashed in on her. She suddenly remembered why, exactly, she hadn't bothered to lower the blinds. In truth, she hadn't pulled the curtains, but someone else had. Probably the same person who had urged her into her bed so their second round of lovemaking could take place in more leisurely comfort.

She sat up, then immediately squealed and sank back under the covers. She was naked. Totally, completely naked. She never slept naked, but then she never brought a man she'd barely met back to her apartment and had sex with him.

Embarrassment heated her cheeks. What had she been thinking? Easy answer—she hadn't. She'd been too busy *feeling*.

But that was no excuse, she told herself as she clutched the sheets to her chest and slowly sat up again. There were no excuses, no way to justify what she'd done. Momentary insanity, she thought glumly. What other explanation could there be?

She glanced around the room, looking for evidence that Carter was still around. There was no noise from the bathroom and she didn't see any of his clothes. Had he left? Would that make things better or worse?

Before she could decide, she spotted a piece of paper resting at the foot of the bed. Cautiously, careful to stay covered by the sheet, she reached for it.

Morning, Rachel. Sorry to duck out without saying goodbye, but I have to be at work really early and I didn't let you get a whole lot of sleep last night, so I didn't want to wake you before dawn. You're amazing and I hope I can see you again. Here's my cell number.

He'd left a phone number and signed his name.

Rachel read the note over a couple of times before setting it on the nightstand. He was gone. That was a relief. She didn't have to deal with any awkward "morning after" conversation. In truth, she didn't have to deal with anything. Last night had been a weird, unexplainable phenomenon. Like a bubble in the space-time continuum. She would accept it as such and move on.

Right, she thought as she got out of bed and ran to the closet so she could pull on her robe. Moving on was an excellent plan. Last night had never even happened. She wouldn't think about it ever again.

Except, as she walked to the kitchen to start her morning coffee, she noticed that specific parts of her felt a little sore. Her hips and thighs had that stretched-too-far ache and there was a faint sort of throb in more intimate places.

No wonder, she thought with a smile. The first time had been all heat and speed, but the second had been incredibly slow and seductive and—

"Stop!" she said aloud in a firm voice. "No thinking, remember? This is thinking. Stop it."

Right. She had to remember it had all been a big mistake. Not one she would ever repeat, under any circumstances. Carter could have been a serial killer. Right now her body could be in chunks all over the place. She'd been stupid and for reasons not clear to anyone, she'd gotten out unscathed.

As for calling Carter, that wasn't going to happen. What was she supposed to say to him? How could she explain she wasn't that type of woman, when as far as he was concerned, she obviously was. She hated that he would think she was slutty, but she couldn't think of a way to change his mind. He was good-looking enough that this sort of thing probably happened to him all the time. He wouldn't even give her another thought, just as she'd get him out of her mind immediately. Starting right now.

But when she reached for her coffeepot, she realized it was full and that the aroma of the fresh brew filled the room.

He'd made coffee before he'd left, she realized with a little sigh. Talk about thoughtful.

The phone rang. Rachel's heart fluttered briefly before she consciously squashed the sensation. No fluttering, no anticipation, no hoping, no Carter. Besides, the man might know where she lived and be on very intimate terms with her body, but he didn't know her phone number.

"Hello?"

"Rachel? It's Diane. Are you okay?"

"I'm fine."

Diane sighed. "I'm so sorry about last night. I can't believe I took off like that and left you. I nearly had a heart attack when I got home and realized what I'd done. I came right back but the bartender said you'd already gotten a ride home. I would have called then, but it seemed so late. Are you sure you're fine?"

"I am," she said, determined to make it true by sheer force of will.

"Okay. Good. Obviously Eddy makes me crazy. I'm

so not going out with him anymore." Diane sighed. "I should be more like you. You're so sensible when it comes to men."

Rachel held in a wince. "I have my moments, like everyone else."

Diane laughed. "Oh, please. When was the last time you did anything impetuous with a guy?"

Rachel wasn't about to answer *that* question. "Thanks for checking on me. I'll see you later at school."

"Right. Bye."

Rachel hung up the phone and poured herself a mug of coffee. It was a new day and she had a new plan. No more wild nights with men she didn't know. She would go back to being the kind of woman Diane assumed she was. Better for everyone, especially herself.

The rhythmic click of the knitting needles was a good memory for Rachel. One of her years in foster care had been with an older woman who had taught her to knit. She associated the feel of the soft yarn and the sound of the needles with calm evenings spent by a fire with plenty of hot cocoa on hand.

"She's going to throw me out of class," Crissy said in a low voice.

Noelle grinned at Rachel, then turned to their friend. "She's not. She likes you."

"Ha. She has to." Crissy tugged at her tangled knitting. "I gave her a free month at one of my gyms. I know it's wrong to bribe people but I didn't know what else to do."

Rachel held in a smile. "Gee, Crissy, have you

thought of actually paying attention to your knitting? It *is* why we're here."

Crissy laughed. "Oh, please. You know I only come here so we can go to dinner afterward. The first set of classes wasn't too bad, but now things are so complicated. Who writes these patterns?"

"We could meet you for dinner after knitting class," Noelle offered.

"This is fine," Crissy told her as she held out her needles to Rachel. "I'll muddle through."

"*Muddle* being the key word," Rachel said as she took the disaster and began unraveling it. "How can you mess up casting on? It's just not that complicated."

"I'm a businesswoman. I can run my company, but I'm not very good with my hands," Crissy said. "Big deal."

Noelle, ever the peacemaker, patted her arm. "You could try a little harder."

"I could also wish to be taller," Crissy said. "It's not happening."

Rachel looked at Noelle. "She's hopeless."

"Pretty much," Noelle said cheerfully. "But we love her anyway."

Noelle set down her needles and stretched her arms above her head. "I'm getting creaky," she said. "I'm only twenty and I'm already stiff and old."

Crissy leaned over and hugged Noelle. "You're pregnant. There's a difference." She patted her friend's round belly. "I can't believe how long it took you to show. You're into your sixth month and you're not big at all."

"I feel big," Noelle said with a contented smile. "I feel huge. But it's good."

"Of course it is," Rachel told her. "How's Dev?"

Noelle's expression turned dreamy. "Perfect in every way. He wants us to go away before the baby's born. Sort of a belated honeymoon. But he doesn't want me to worry about flying. So he's been looking into a cruise on the Mexican Riviera. Maybe in late January."

Rachel couldn't help smiling at her friend. Noelle radiated happiness. Her marriage to Devlin Hunter had started out as a purely practical arrangement that had turned into something wonderful when they'd fallen in love. Even their brief scare that something might be wrong with the baby had ended well when the tests had come back with the good news that everything was fine.

Noelle tucked her blond hair behind her ears. "So, what's new with you two?" she asked.

Crissy laughed. "Since last week? Gee, nothing. What about you, Rach? Any deep, dark secrets you want to share?"

"Not really," Rachel murmured. She was still a little sore from her wild adventure three nights before, but she sure wasn't going to mention that to her friends. While she didn't think they would actually disapprove, she wasn't ready to confess all. Maybe she never would be.

In truth, she couldn't figure out why she'd allowed things to get so out-of-hand with Carter. Okay, he'd been funny and charming and sexy. In her line of work, she didn't meet a lot of guys like that. Most of the men in her circle were married and fathers of five-year-olds.

And yes, it had been long time since her last relationship, so maybe she'd been in a weakened condition. But still—that was hardly an excuse for what she'd done.

Just as bad, she was starting to regret throwing away Carter's note, which was crazy. It wasn't as if she would have ever called the man. And say what? Invite him out on a date? He would think she was only interested in him for sex. How humiliating. Not that she wasn't interested in him that way, but there would have to be more than just that. Just thinking about it all was confusing, which meant that a relationship would be difficult and if there were this many questions now, what was the point?

She knew better than to get involved. Caring meant losing and she'd already had enough pain in her life.

"Earth to Rachel," Noelle said. "Are you all right?"

"What? Oh." Rachel handed Crissy her knitting project. "I'm fine. Just a little distracted."

"I would normally assume work," Crissy said, "but you had the oddest look on your face."

Rachel willed herself not to blush. "It's nothing."

Crissy didn't look convinced. "I make it a rule never to pry, but I'm tempted this one time. Just promise me you won't do what Noelle did and turn up pregnant."

"Of course not," Rachel said. "I'm not dating anyone."

"Dating isn't actually required," Crissy informed her with a grin. "Sometimes proximity is enough."

Noelle laughed. Rachel forced herself to smile, despite the dark, ugly pit that had opened up in her stomach.

Pregnant? No! It wasn't possible. No, no, no. She couldn't be. They'd only done it those two times. Just twice.

Without protection.

Rachel wanted to run screaming into the early evening. She wanted to pound her head against the table, or at the very least, turn back time and not invite Carter into her apartment that night.

She couldn't be pregnant. She was single and a kindergarten teacher. This wasn't part of her plan. Not yet. Of course she wanted a husband and a family, just like most women. But in that order. Someday. When she was feeling brave enough to risk her heart.

It wasn't possible, she told herself firmly, fighting the need to throw up. She would be fine.

Seventeen days after her night with Carter and fourteen days after considering the possibility of pregnancy, Rachel sat on the edge of her tub and told herself not to break into hysterics.

She'd waited an extra two days just to be sure. She'd been patient, she'd done her best not to think about it. She'd willed her period to start exactly on time and when it hadn't, she'd gone the extra mile just to be sure.

Now, she stared at the seven plastic sticks she'd neatly lined up on two paper towels. They were from three different kits and they all said exactly the same thing.

Positively pregnant.

Chapter Three

Rachel hadn't planned on ever returning to the Blue Dog Bar. Unfortunately, since she'd tossed the note with Carter's cell number on it, she had no way to get in touch with the man. But she had remembered that one of the bartenders—Rachel couldn't remember her name—had known Carter well enough to have his number and so here she was, showing up at three-thirty in the afternoon, with a nervous stomach and several spots of drying paste on the hem of her skirt.

Kindergarteners were hard on their teacher's clothes, she thought as she glanced down at the dark patches. At least the paste would wash out. If only her problem with Carter could be solved as easily.

She drew in a deep breath, wished she hadn't been

so hasty with that note he'd left and walked into the dim building.

It was early enough that there weren't many customers. Rachel ignored the few patrons and made her way to the bar, where she sighed in relief when she recognized the same woman who had been here that night three weeks ago.

The woman behind the bar smiled. "Hi. Can I help you?" She was pretty—late twenties, with a cute, short haircut and big green eyes.

"I hope so," Rachel said, wishing she weren't so nervous. She could feel herself shaking. "I'm, ah, looking for Carter."

The bartender continued to smile. "Okay. Carter who?"

Rachel held in a moan of humiliation. "I don't know," she admitted in a rush. "I met him here three weeks ago. I didn't mean to. I was here with a friend and she was breaking up with this guy and…" She sucked in a breath and clutched the large envelope of papers to her chest. "That's not important, right? Because no one cares. Okay. We, ah, met and I need to talk to him. It's really important. Carter. He's about six-two with dark blond hair and a diamond stud earring."

Honestly, how many Carters could there be? Rachel swallowed hard, then blurted out, "He has a scar shaped like a lightning bolt on his thigh right by his…"

"Oh," the woman said, knowing. "*That* Carter. Have a seat. I'll see if I can get in touch with him."

Carter couldn't decide if he was annoyed or relieved. He couldn't believe it had been three weeks and Rachel was only now getting in touch with him. Sure, hard-to-get was a time-honored game between the sexes, but hey—it was him. He'd never had to wait to get a call before.

Logically, this was probably better. He knew better than to get involved and if she were the kind of female totally into games, he wouldn't be into her. Problem solved.

Except he had a feeling it wouldn't be that simple. He hadn't been able to get Rachel out of his mind. He knew where she lived and could have gone to see her, but that wasn't his style. Besides, he'd left her his number and she hadn't called. What did that say about what she thought about him?

He walked into the Blue Dog Bar determined to make her want him, even though he didn't know if he wanted her. His male pride was at stake. He nodded at Jenny, who pointed to a booth in the back. He squared his shoulders and strolled casually in that direction.

Only to get broadsided by a two-by-four.

It didn't matter that the hunk of wood was metaphorical. His gut twisted, the air rushed out of his lungs and he would swear he could hear angels singing. Damn, she looked good.

Rachel sat facing the bar, her back all straight, her clothes prissy enough for a preacher's wife and her hair tied back in some kind of fancy braid. But he knew the truth. He knew that behind that don't-touch-me-I'm-a-good-girl exterior beat the heart of a wanton. She kissed like a dream and made love as if it were her last time.

Heat poured through him and he had a brief but

intense fantasy about dragging her onto the table and taking her right there. Only he'd never been one to show off in front of strangers. Besides, she hadn't called and that might have hurt his feelings.

"Rachel," he said as he approached.

She half stood, then sank back into the seat. "Hello, Carter."

He slid into the seat across from her, then noticed the large legal-sized envelope she'd placed on the table. What was that about?

"It's been awhile," he said.

She nodded. "Three weeks."

She licked her lips, which made his whole body clench. Damn, why did she have to get to him?

She put her hands on the table, laced her fingers together, then pulled back and dropped them to her lap. Nervousness radiated from her like a fine mist. He half expected her to clutch her stomach and run for the bathroom.

He'd decided to play it cool, to let her do all the talking. Not only was it a power play, but he would learn more that way. So he got really annoyed with himself when he blurted out, "You didn't call."

She blinked at him. "Excuse me?"

"You didn't call. I was polite. I had to be up early and I didn't want to wake you, so I left a note. And my phone number." He leaned toward her. "I don't go home with just anyone. Is that what you thought? You could use me and forget about me?"

He swore silently. Had those words come out of his

mouth? If anyone ever found out he'd said them, he would be drummed out of the male gender and forced to live as a eunuch.

Her eyes widened. "I didn't use you."

"What would you call it? You had your way with me and then walked away without a second thought." Until today, but he doubted she would think of that.

"I'm the woman. I can't use you," she said.

"Right. Because only guys can be jerks. Women always act perfectly."

"Well, no. Of course not." She stared at him. "I wasn't trying to use you."

"You could have called."

"I didn't know what to say."

"How about 'Thanks for the great night. We should go out sometime.'" Unless she hadn't wanted to go out with him again, which wasn't possible.

She drew in a deep breath. "Carter, I'm sorry I didn't call, but we have something else more important to discuss."

Important, huh? With women, that generally meant one thing. The relationship. But he and Rachel didn't have a relationship.

"I'm listening," he said.

She nodded, then exhaled. "There are ramifications from our night together."

It took a second for her words to sink in. He swore under his breath and felt all desire bleed from his body.

"If you have something, you should have told me," he growled.

Dammit all to hell, he had no one but himself to blame. He hadn't used anything and he knew better. Not that he usually traveled with a condom. But he should have stopped to think, to ask, to be a responsible adult.

How bad was it? Would his…would it fall off?

"What?" she asked, sounding slightly outraged. "*Have something?* I'm not sick. There's nothing wrong with me."

"There's nothing wrong with me, either," he told her. "I'm fine. So if we're both fine, what's the problem?"

She glared at him. "Seeing you know everything about women, you should have already figured it out. I'm pregnant."

Had he mentioned that all of his trouble came from the women in his life? Timing being what it was, Jenny chose that moment to come up and ask if they wanted something to drink.

He looked up at her and sighed. "Give us a minute," he said.

"Sure thing."

Jenny glanced at Rachel and then headed back to the bar.

Carter knew what would happen next. He figured they had maybe fifteen minutes more of privacy and, given the topic, they were going to need a lot more.

He turned his attention back to Rachel and let her words wash over him. Pregnant. *Pregnant?*

"You're not on the Pill?" he asked, more to himself than her. Because he hadn't asked before…when it had mattered.

"No," she said, her voice low and annoyed.

"You let yourself have sex with me without protection or birth control?"

She opened her mouth and then closed it. "Not on purpose," she told him. "It wasn't as if I'd planned the night. It just sort of happened. I lost my head."

And that was going to be his fault.

"I don't do this sort of thing very much," she said, obviously still annoyed, although he couldn't figure out what *her* problem was. He was the injured party here.

"Meaning?" he asked.

She glanced around, then lowered her voice. "I've only been with two other guys and I was engaged to both of them."

"You've been married before?" he asked, feeling slightly outraged. "Twice?"

"No." She leaned back against the seat and groaned. "I was engaged, not married. That isn't the point. I'm pregnant."

"I got that."

"There's going to be a baby."

That stopped him. Because until she'd said the "b" word, he hadn't put the two together. Pregnant was a scary, dangerous condition used to trap men, but a baby was something pretty miraculous.

He felt himself smile. "Yeah?"

"Don't you dare be happy," she told him. "Neither

of us planned this. We don't even know each other." She thrust the envelope toward him. "I've been to a lawyer. This is a very straightforward agreement. I'm not asking you for anything now or ever. In return, you sign away all rights to the child."

"Why would I do that?"

She rolled her eyes. "Because it makes the most sense. Like I said, we barely know each other. We can't have a baby together."

"I'd say we already are."

From the corner of his eye, he saw Jenny on the phone. She was quick, he would give her that.

A baby. He didn't know what he felt, exactly, except a certainty that the kid would be a girl. As for signing away his rights, that wasn't going to happen in this lifetime.

"We need to talk," he said, then winced. Was Jenny spiking the beer? Was he turning into a woman?

"There's nothing to talk about. You should look at the papers."

He leaned toward her. "I'm not discussing this in a bar."

She flinched. "I'm not taking you home with me. Look what happened last time."

He wanted to tell her that he wasn't interested in her that way—except he was. Now that he knew all his parts were going to stay in place, he could appreciate her pale skin and the way her mouth curved when she smiled. Not that she'd done so in recent memory.

"I'm not trying to sleep with you," he said. "We can go to my place. Follow me in your car. Keep the damn engine running if you want. My point is, I'm not talking about this here."

He didn't mention that his ex-girlfriend was still friends with his mother and likely on the phone with her this exact second. Hence the need for speed.

Rachel considered his words, then nodded slowly. "Fine. Your place. But I want you to consider my offer. I'm not trying to trap you."

"Good to know."

Rachel enjoyed her little convertible and she'd always liked driving the manual transmission. Only this afternoon she couldn't stop shaking, which made it difficult to shift.

The conversation with Carter hadn't gone at all the way she'd imagined. For one thing, he'd kept talking about the fact that she hadn't called him. As if he'd wanted her to.

Honestly, the thought had never crossed her mind. She'd figured he slept with different women all the time and one more wasn't going to make an impact on his life. Had she been wrong? Did he really care that she hadn't called?

The thought was so foreign, she didn't know how to process it in her brain. Adding to the confusion was his refusal to instantly sign off on the baby. She'd never thought he would *want* to take on that kind of responsibility. Weren't women always complaining that men hated the idea of being tied down?

She had to make him understand they weren't in this

together. Dealing with being pregnant was hard enough, and not something she'd even begun to accept, but having to deal with Carter, too, was unimaginable.

She followed his large, black truck into a pleasant neighborhood, the kind populated by young families. When he pulled into the driveway of a pretty, one-story house, she parked in front and climbed out.

For a second, she looked around and felt herself get lost in the past. This was the sort of street where she'd grown up. Modest homes filled with parents and kids and lots of laughter. Even after all these years, she could remember everything about her old bedroom. The color of the wallpaper, the bookshelves on the wall, the way her mother would tease her about the mess on the floor.

Happy memories, she thought wistfully. Happy and so very, very sad.

"Rachel?"

She looked up and saw Carter waiting by the front door. She walked up the path and into his house.

The living room was open, with cream-colored drapes and pretty sage paint on the walls. The furniture looked relatively new and not the least bit like bachelor leather.

"Have a seat," he said, closing the front door behind her. "You want something to drink?"

"I'm fine."

She set the paperwork on the coffee table, then sank on the sofa. Now what?

Apparently Carter didn't know, either. He paced the length of the room, paused in front of her, started to speak, shook his head and started pacing again. She reminded herself that she'd had several days to attempt to get used to the news and she still wasn't dealing with it. The poor man would need some time.

"I didn't plan this," she said by way of a peace offering. "I want you to know that. What happened between us was totally unexpected."

He looked at her and smiled. "I know. I was there."

Somehow, she found herself getting lost in his brown eyes. She felt a pull between them. Something strong and powerful that made her want to stand up and step into his arms. Once there he would draw her close and…

Whoa! That's what had gotten her in trouble in the first place, she thought.

She cleared her throat. "My point is, I don't want you to be concerned. I can take care of myself." She wasn't sure how yet and thinking about being a single mother made her hyperventilate, but that wasn't his problem. "I have no intention of trapping you. You can take as long as you'd like to look over the papers."

His expression hardened. "Let's get this clear right now. I'm not signing away my kid."

He couldn't mean that. "Do you want to be a father?"

"I didn't plan on it this week, no. But we're talking about my child." He gave a strangled laugh. "Who am I kidding? My daughter. And you can't have her."

He stopped and put his hands on his hips. From her seated position, he looked very powerful and masculine and just a little intimidating.

"You can't mean that," she murmured, as caught off

guard by his presence as by his words. "I never thought you'd be interested. You don't know me."

"Knowledge isn't required. We did it, it happened, now we'll deal with it."

What he said sounded perfectly logical, but this was not the conversation she thought they'd be having.

But before she could say that, the front door burst open and three women entered. One was in her fifties, the others were about Carter's age. Rachel stood and stared at them.

Carter groaned. "Mama, this is not a good time."

"You're one to talk about timing," the older woman said, pushing past him to stand in front of Rachel. "A man who gets a woman pregnant without meaning to should talk about timing. Apparently he's very good at it."

Mama? As in…his mother?

She was about five foot two, with short blond hair and Carter's eyes. Tiny, but Rachel could feel the energy pouring off her. The other two women were taller and pretty, but they were a little intimidating, too.

"H-how did you know?" she asked, not sure she wanted the answer.

Carter slumped into one of the club chairs opposite the sofa. "Jenny called her. Rachel, this is my mother, Nina Brockett, and two of my sisters, Liz and Merry. You don't need to know who is who because they won't be staying. Mama, this is Rachel."

"Of course we're staying," his mother told him, then turned to Rachel. "You should sit."

"Why would the bartender call you?" Rachel asked, wondering if this would ever make sense.

"Jenny's a friend of the family," Nina told her.

"We stay in touch with most of Carter's old girl-friends," one of his sisters offered. "There have been lots, but you're the first one to get pregnant."

Jenny from the bar was his *ex-girlfriend?*

"She's married," Carter said, as if he could read her mind. "I doubt you can make your escape now. You might as well sit."

"Of course she should sit," Nina said, moving next to Rachel, taking her hand and urging her back on the sofa. "She needs to rest. She's going to have a baby."

"The baby is maybe four cells big," Carter told her. "I doubt it's going to tire her out."

Rachel looked at him. "You went out with Jenny?" she asked, feeling herself blush. "She pretended not to know who you were. She made me describe…"

She suddenly became aware of the other three women in the room and sank onto the sofa.

"It doesn't matter," she whispered.

"That Jenny has a real sense of humor," Carter muttered.

One of the sisters smiled. "She's great. Carter was an usher in her wedding and she was a bridesmaid in mine."

This was way too much information, Rachel thought frantically, glancing at the door and wondering if she could make a run for it. This wasn't happening. She hadn't just met Carter's mother, two sisters *and* his ex-girlfriend.

Nina patted her hand. "You'll be fine. This is shocking now, but that's because Carter didn't tell you about us. Why my only son wouldn't mention his family to the mother of his child, I don't know. But I'm *only* the mother. No one tells me anything."

"Save me," Carter muttered as he rubbed his temples. "Mama, you're not helping."

"Of course I'm helping," his mother insisted. "I want to help. It's what I do best. So, what were the two of you talking about when we got here?"

Rachel glanced at the envelope on the table. Suddenly Carter's unwillingness to walk away from his unborn child made a little more sense.

"That's private," Carter told her.

"You might as well tell us," one of his sisters said. "We'll find out anyway."

"No, you won't," Carter told her. He looked at Rachel. "If you want to make a run for it, I'll cover your back."

"She's not running," Nina said and it was only then Rachel realized the older woman still had a firm grip on her hand.

Rachel tugged it free. "Carter and I have some things we need to work out," she said weakly.

"Of course you do." Nina smiled at her. "You're a nice girl, I can tell. You didn't mean to get pregnant. But it happens. So we'll deal with it."

We? No, no. There was no *we*. "Technically, I'm the one who's pregnant," she began.

Carter's gaze narrowed. "And I'm the father."

"I'm not denying that," Rachel said, bristling. "I'm the one who came to you."

"I would have been happy to do things the other way," he reminded her. "You didn't call."

The sisters looked at each other. "Really? You went out with Carter and didn't call the next day?" one of them asked.

"Ah…"

"The women always call," the other sister said. "Some of them won't stop calling."

"Ah…"

"It gets embarrassing," the first one continued. "I want to take them aside and tell them to have a little pride."

"It's not their fault," Nina said with a proud smile. "It's my son."

Rachel raised her eyebrows. "Really?"

Carter groaned. "Ignore them. I mean that."

"Maybe I want to hear about 'the women.'"

"You don't," he told her. "Trust me."

"About the baby," Nina said, breaking the mood. "We need to talk." Nina patted the back of her hand. "I understand. If you young people insist on putting the cart before the horse, then they need to turn the horse around."

"What?" Rachel and Carter asked together.

Nina glanced between them. "Isn't it obvious? You have a baby coming. You need to get married."

Chapter Four

Carter stood. He'd been willing to let the moment run its course. Thirty years of being his mother's son had taught him that was the easiest way to deal with her. He would listen and then do exactly what he wanted. But mother or not, she'd just crossed the line.

"Okay, that's enough," he said flatly and walked to the door. "Great to see you all. Thanks for stopping by."

His mother was about a foot shorter, but that never seemed to bother her. She rose and walked over until she was in front of him, staring up, glaring.

"Carter Brockett, I'm serious."

"So am I, Mama. This isn't about you. This is between me and Rachel. We're going to deal with it and we don't need your help."

Her brown eyes narrowed. "You're going to have a baby, Carter. This is serious."

He knew she meant well. He knew she loved him and would gladly throw herself in front of a train for him. But sometimes she was the biggest pain in the butt.

He bent down and kissed her. "I know, Mama. Trust me, okay?"

She sighed heavily, then nodded. As she stepped out of the house, his sisters trailed after her. Merry grinned.

"You're in big trouble, now," she murmured as she passed.

"Thanks for the support."

"Any time."

He closed the door behind them.

Rachel still sat on the sofa, although she looked a little shell-shocked. His family had that effect on people. He'd seen it many times.

He walked into the kitchen and got her a glass of ice water, then returned to the living room. She stared at him, her green eyes wide, her mouth slightly parted.

"You doing okay?" he asked.

"No." She took the glass he offered. "Who *were* those people?"

He sank back into his chair. "My family. Most of them, anyway. I have another sister around somewhere. She must not have been home or she would have been part of the parade, too."

"You have three sisters, right?"

"I'm the youngest and the only boy. My dad died before I was born so it was just me and them. A world of women."

She sipped the water. "When you said women were the cause of all the trouble in your life, I thought you meant romantically."

"That would have made things too easy. I'm surrounded by them. Even my dog, a stray Lab who showed up one day all skinny and pathetic, is female. Welcome to my world."

She managed a small smile. "It's not so bad. Your family obviously cares about you." She took another drink. "Did Jenny really call your mother to tell her what she'd heard?"

"Oh, yeah. Jenny stayed pretty tight with her and my sisters. As have a lot of my ex-girlfriends. They show up at holidays or parties. I never know when I'm going to run into one." Or twenty, he thought grimly. Why couldn't his ex-girlfriends be like other women? Bitter and vindictive. Right now the idea of someone slashing his tires was a whole lot easier to deal with than someone like Jenny, who simply stayed in his world.

Not that he didn't like Jenny—he did. She'd married a great guy, but damn, whose side was she on? Calling his mother and telling her Rachel was pregnant.

Rachel set down her glass and glanced at him. "I didn't get pregnant on purpose."

"I know. Neither of us planned on that. We just weren't thinking."

She ducked her head, but he saw her smile. "I was kind of swept away. Nothing like that has ever happened to me before."

"Me, either."

She looked up and rolled her eyes. "Oh, please. I might not know you very well, but I'm getting a clear idea about your past. You seem to have women lined up around the block."

"Sure, a lot of relationships, but that kind of heat?" He shrugged, trying to remember the last time he'd felt it. "It doesn't happen very often."

"Are you just saying that?"

The uncertainty in her voice added to her charm. They were already in so much trouble, Carter almost felt still being attracted to her couldn't make things worse. Except he knew it could. A relationship would only complicate the situation. Better to keep his head and think clearly. If only she didn't smell so good.

"I don't do lines," he told her. "You're beautiful and sexy and funny. You dress like a nun and you have a body made for…ah, making love," he said, self-editing to something less graphic. "What's not to like?"

"Wow. When you say it like that, you were lucky to have me."

He smiled. "Yes, I was. Only now there are consequences for us to deal with."

"The baby."

"Right. Rachel, I'm not giving up my daughter."

"You don't actually know the baby is a girl."

"Yes, I do, but that doesn't matter. We're going to have to work something out, because I won't sign those papers."

He'd understood why she'd thought he might. Many

guys would jump at the chance to walk away from this kind of responsibility, but he couldn't. He'd been raised to believe family mattered more than anything.

She leaned forward and fingered the thick envelope. "I know. I mean I didn't know before, but I do now." She straightened and touched her stomach. "So what do we do? No offense, but I'm not going to accept your mother's suggestion."

"You don't want to marry me?" he asked, his voice teasing.

"I don't know you."

"I'm a great catch."

"You certainly don't seem to have an ego problem."

He grinned. "I have references."

"Apparently in the hundreds."

"Not that many." He stood and moved to the sofa, where he angled toward her. "How about this. We have what, eight months until the baby is born?"

"Just about."

"Okay, let's take that time and figure out what we want to do. Not what my mother says is best. We'll talk about the situation and come up with a plan." He hesitated. "You're going to keep the baby, aren't you?"

She stiffened. "Of course. I want this child."

"Me, too. So what do you say? We'll take our time and consider our options. You live in the area, I live in the area, we could easily share custody. Or figure out something else that works. Let's get to know each other and find out what works best for us."

She bit her lower lip, which made him think about

doing that for her, which made him think about other things. They *were* alone in the house.

Only that wasn't a very good idea right now.

"You're right," she said, obviously oblivious to the temptation she represented. "We have time. We should use it."

"Great." He grabbed a pen and paper from the end table and wrote down his home and cell number. Then he held the sheet out to her. "You're not going to throw it out again, are you?"

"No, I promise I won't."

She reached for the paper, but he held it out of reach. "Why didn't you call me?"

She sighed. "Are you ever going to let that go?"

"Probably not until you answer the question."

She sank back against the sofa. "I couldn't call you, Carter. I honestly didn't know what to say. I'd never done anything like that in my life. I was afraid of what you'd think of me. And I was afraid of what I'd think of myself."

He dropped the paper in her lap and gave an exaggerated sigh. "I knew it. You were just using me for sex."

She groaned. "You're impossible."

"Sometimes I'm even better than that."

"Give me those."

She reached across the sofa and grabbed the pen and paper from him. Suddenly they were very close, with her breasts pressing against his arm and one of her hands lightly touching his stomach.

His reaction was instant and predictable. Blood

rushed south, and his brain went blank, except for the burning need to pull her into his arms.

Her gaze locked with his and he was gratified to see an answering fire there. Unfortunately, she had more self-control.

"I'll, ah, give you my number," she murmured as she drew back and quickly wrote down the information. "We should plan to get together and talk some more."

"How about Saturday?" he asked.

She handed him back the pad. "Okay. Do you want to go out or…" She shook her head. "No matter what I say, it's going to sound like a date."

"It's not a date," he told her, suddenly wishing it was. "Let's go casual. I'll bring dinner to your place. That way we won't be interrupted."

She blinked several times.

"While we talk," he added, emphasizing the last word. "Just talk."

"Okay. That's fine. We'll talk."

Carter went out back and whistled for Goldie. The golden Lab, named by one of his nieces, strolled out of her plush doghouse, stretched and ambled toward him. She gave him a quick lick on the hand by way of greeting, then bumped her head against his thigh so he would rub her ears.

"Have you noticed everything in this relationship is about you?" he asked conversationally as he obliged her for a couple of minutes. "Come on. We're going to see Mama."

The magic name perked up Goldie and she trotted eagerly to the side gate. Carter let her out, then followed her down the street. Goldie paused at the curb until he'd checked for traffic, then dashed across to a tidy front yard. She sniffed the big tree in front, raced up the two steps, rose on her back legs and pressed her paw against the bell.

The front door opened and his mother appeared.

"Goldie. Such a pretty dog. Come in, come in. I have some nice pot roast from last night. I saved you some." His mother held open the screen door for the dog, then glanced at him. "If you're going to tell me to mind my own business, you can go home now."

"That's exactly what I'm going to tell you and you know you'd never send me away without feeding me first."

"You think you know everything," his mother grumbled, but held the screen door open for him, too, then shooed him into the kitchen.

Carter had grown up in this house. He'd painted walls, laid tile and, when he was nine, broken the front window with a high fly ball hit from Billy Hinton's front yard. There were a lot of memories under this roof. Mostly good ones.

The kitchen was large and open, with painted cabinets and a six-burner stove that was always in use. Right now marinara sauce bubbled away.

He glanced around at the table. "Where are the girls?" He'd expected an inquisition.

"I sent them home. I wanted to talk to you alone."

That was never good news, he thought glumly as he pulled up a stool at the island and took a cookie from the ever-present plate of them. Neither the alone part nor her confidence that he would stop by.

"I appreciate your interest," he told his mother. "I love you, but stay out of this. Rachel and I have to figure out what to do ourselves."

"What to do?"

His mother might be short, but she was formidable when she got her back up. Right now, with him on the stool, they were perilously close to eye level. She glared at him.

"*What to do?*" she repeated, sounding both outraged and furious. "If you get a girl pregnant, Carter, you marry her. I raised you to know that."

There was something mythic about his mother. Carter had never figured out the source of her power, but he respected it. With the right look and tone of voice, she could make him feel as if he were ten years old again.

"Things have changed," he said. "Lots of women have babies on their own. That's what Rachel wants to do." The woman had tried to get him to sign away his own child. Nothing about those actions indicated a burning desire to marry him.

"Did you propose? Did you offer to take responsibility?"

"I said I wanted to be a part of my child's life. I want to share custody with her."

His mother walked to the sink, where she began rinsing pots. "Share custody. What does that mean? Half a life with a child? You're having a baby, Carter. This isn't a game. You have to marry this girl."

"She doesn't want to marry me."

"How do you know? Have you asked?"

He didn't mention the legal paperwork. She wouldn't understand a woman expecting a man to walk away from a child and it might make her dislike Rachel. Nina Brockett was a wonderful woman, but she could hold a grudge for decades. Better to take the fall himself. After all, Rachel was going to be his baby's mother, so there would be plenty of contact between Rachel and *his* mother.

"I already know the answer," he said.

"You think you do, but you could be wrong. Stranger things have happened."

"Mama, give it a rest."

She flung down a dishcloth and spun to face him. "I won't give it a rest. You're my son. We're talking about your firstborn child. You have to be a father to that baby."

He put down the cookie. "I'm going to be," he said quietly. "I'll be there."

Her expression softened. "I know, Carter. I'm sorry. You know more than anyone what it's like to grow up without a father."

"Then trust me to do the right thing," he said.

"I can't even trust you to wear a condom."

Every now and then she surprised the hell out of him. Desperate to escape he looked around for Goldie, who was nosing the now licked-clean dish on the floor by the pantry.

"I gotta go," he said as he stood, then whistled for his dog.

"Marry the girl."

"I love you, Mama."

"I love you, too. I'd love you more if you'd marry Rachel."

"Good to know."

He let himself out and made his way back to his house, knowing he could run but he couldn't hide. Once his mother had something lodged in her brain, she never let it go. She would be all over him until he and Rachel had tied the knot.

The thing was he didn't object to marriage in theory…for other people. But honestly, he didn't see the point. Why be with one person forever?

His sisters kept telling him he didn't understand because he'd never been in love. That one day he would fall and fall hard, and they all couldn't wait to be there.

He told them hell would freeze over first, but he hadn't meant it. He wouldn't mind falling in love. He wanted to feel that he couldn't live without the one person who made him want to get up every morning. Only he'd never found anyone who came close to that. Eventually he'd decided that romantic love was a myth—a product of greeting card advertisers.

If Rachel had wanted to get married to give the baby his name, he probably would have said yes, as long as she understood he wasn't about to fall in love with her. But from what he'd seen, that was the last thing on her mind. So they would work something out—a sensible plan that took care of all their needs and the baby's as well. Because he knew one thing for sure—he might not believe in romantic love, but he knew about a parent's love for a child and no one was going to keep him from that.

"I'm having wine," Crissy said as they took their seats in the restaurant after knitting class. "I need it. I swear, I have an anti-knitting gene. If it wasn't that I wanted to hang out with you two so much, I would have given up that first week."

"You're not that bad," Noelle said kindly.

"Jan flinched when I showed her what I'd done. Did you see that?" Crissy asked, then shook her head. "I know you're going to want to take the advanced class and she's never going to let me. She'll probably hire a security guard just to keep me out."

Rachel laughed. "I don't think she cares that much. You're doing fine."

Crissy picked up her menu. "You mean you're able to rework what I've messed up and it looks okay." She shook her head. "I need to let it go. I'm a good person with a successful career."

"And a really nice car," Noelle added.

"Very upscale," Rachel said, remembering the too-cute coupe her friend had leased that week.

"I have good friends," Crissy said. "That should be enough, right? I don't date, but that's by choice. Another first date is the last thing I need. So I'm good. I can let the knitting thing go."

"Let it fly free," Rachel told her. "The yarn will thank you."

Noelle chuckled. Crissy rolled her eyes. "It's not my fault," she muttered as she opened her menu. "I hate the yarn."

"It knows," Rachel said, hiding her smile. "It knows and it flinches when it sees you coming."

Crissy set down her menu and leaned across the table. "It's not fair. I have absolutely no crafty or home-making type talents."

Rachel thought of her friend's minichain of women-only gyms. She'd opened her fourth the previous year and was looking at locations for a fifth.

"Want to trade paychecks?" Rachel asked brightly.

Crissy grinned. "Thanks, but no. You do a good thing, teaching those little kids, and you'll get your reward in heaven. Mine is more immediate."

"That's okay," Rachel assured her. "I've always wanted to be a kindergarten teacher." She'd planned to dance for ten or fifteen years, then go teach. As it was, the teaching had started a little early.

Crissy picked up her menu. "What are we all having? Rachel, have some wine, please. I hate to drink alone and Noelle is obviously out of the running on that."

Rachel opened her mouth, then closed it. She wasn't sure what to say, or how. Of course she'd planned on telling her friends about the baby, but now? Like this?

Noelle glanced at her. "Are you all right? You've been a little quiet all evening."

"I'm good," Rachel said.

Crissy smiled. "So what's going on? It had to be

something, because I know you're not pregnant like this one here."

Rachel drew in a breath. "Actually, I am."

Noelle's eyes widened. "Rachel, are you serious? Really? That's so great."

Crissy blinked twice, then raised her arm. "Waiter, I need a margarita here. Right away." She lowered her arm. "Pregnant? As in 'with child'? Are you sure?"

Rachel nodded. "I peed on seven sticks. It was quite the event."

"So there's a guy," Crissy said. "There has to be a guy. But I didn't know you were seeing anyone." She looked at Noelle. "Did you know?"

"No." Noelle glanced between them. "She's right. There's a guy. So who is he?"

"A complicated question," Rachel admitted.

The waiter appeared with Crissy's drink. They placed their food order and when he was gone, Noelle leaned forward and rested her forearms on the table.

"Spill," she said.

Rachel sipped her water. "Okay, I'll tell you, but please don't judge me. I never do this sort of thing. I don't date much and I never ever sleep with a guy right away."

Crissy picked up her drink. "You slept with a guy on the first date? Wow—my respect was linked to your ability to knit and hang out with little kids, but this is even better. Tell everything. Start at the beginning and talk slowly."

Rachel explained about going to the bar with Diane and how Carter bought her a drink and that they got to talking. She detailed Diane driving off without her and that Carter had offered her a lift.

"It was supposed to just be a good-night kiss," Rachel admitted. "I never expected to lose control like that."

"It must have been some kiss," Crissy said.

Rachel willed herself not to blush. "We, ah, got swept away. Like in the movies. He left the next morning for an early meeting. He wrote me a note and gave me his phone number."

Noelle folded her arms over her chest. "You've been going out all this time and never told us?"

"We haven't been dating," Rachel said.

Crissy sipped her drink. "You met a guy who kisses so great you were compelled to have sex with him and you're not dating?"

"I didn't call him."

"Why not?" Noelle and Crissy asked together.

Rachel moved her fork around on her napkin. "I don't know. I didn't know what to say. I mean, what would he think of me after that night we'd spent together? I'm not really that kind of person."

Crissy rolled her eyes. "You didn't call him because you thought he'd think you were slutty." She paused. "Do we still say 'slutty'? Am I dating myself?"

"You're doing fine," Noelle told her, then turned to Rachel. "I know you'd feel awkward, but why wouldn't you want to see him again?"

Rachel honestly didn't have an answer. Now that she'd talked to Carter again, even under really difficult circumstances, she'd seen that she liked him, even without the sex thing.

"It's complicated," she said. "I thought avoiding him was for the best."

"But then you turned up pregnant," Crissy said. "That had to have been an interesting conversation. Or have you told him yet."

"I told him," she said. "Actually, first I went to a lawyer."

She explained about the paperwork she'd had drawn up.

Noelle gasped. "Did he sign it? Did he really sign away his baby?"

"No," Rachel admitted. "He refused. I think he was kind of insulted I'd even asked. Then his mother and two of his sisters walked in and they know I'm pregnant."

Crissy and Noelle exchanged a confused look. "Where did his mother come from?" Crissy asked.

Rachel explained about meeting at the bar and Jenny and then following Carter home.

"His mother thinks we should get married."

"She's right," Noelle said primly. "You're having a baby together. It's the right thing to do."

"It's a new century," Crissy said. "No one has to get married anymore. At least not here. Rachel, honey, you do whatever you want. If that means being a single mom, then yay you."

"Work isn't a problem," she said slowly. "One of the other teachers got pregnant and had a baby last year and she's not married."

Noelle leaned forward. "Of course you can be a single parent if you want to be, but isn't that the question? Do you *want* to do this on your own? Dev and I had a marriage of convenience and look how that turned out."

"You're the one in a million," Crissy said. "Rachel, you don't have to marry a complete stranger."

"Actually he's not a complete stranger," Noelle said smugly. "She's seen him naked."

"There is that," Crissy said. "What do you want?"

Rachel sighed. "I don't know. Carter and I have agreed to get to know each other and then figure things out. And don't forget, the marriage was his mother's idea, not his. He never mentioned it at all."

"What would you have said if he had?" Noelle asked.

"I don't know that, either," she admitted. She thought about her conversation with Carter. "Do I dress like a nun?"

Noelle had been drinking her water and now she choked as she tried not to spit. "What?"

"My clothes. I try to dress low-key for the kids. Plus I need things that are washable. But do I dress…I don't know…too conservative?"

Crissy eyed her short-sleeved blouse and long skirt. "You're not on the fashion cutting edge, but you always look nice. Who said you dressed like a nun?"

Rachel shrugged.

"Carter," Crissy said knowingly.

"He didn't mean it in a bad way," Rachel told her. "He was talking about finding me attractive, even though I dress like a nun."

"She's defending him," Noelle said conversationally. "That's step one."

"It's not step anything," Rachel said. "I'm explaining."

"Oooh, step two," Crissy teased. Then her smile faded. "Look, you have to do what feels right for you, Rachel. Whether it's your clothes or your job or your baby. It *is* your baby, so don't let anyone else make the decisions for you."

"It's also Carter's baby," Noelle said gently. "He sounds like a man who wants to be a father."

"He is," Rachel said, more confused than ever. "Plus there's his whole family. They seem really nice."

The kind of family she remembered hers being. Could she be a part of that now? Under these circumstances?

"Carter said we should take our time," Rachel told him. "We're going to meet and talk and figure it all out."

"Sounds like a sensible plan to me," Crissy said. "Just don't be rash."

"I don't do rash," Rachel said.

"All evidence to the contrary," Crissy said, with a pointed glance at Rachel's midsection.

"Okay. Just that one time. My point is, in one way or another I've been on my own since I was twelve. I know how to take care of myself."

"Maybe that's not the issue," Noelle said. "Now there's going to be someone else."

"A baby," Rachel murmured. "I'm still having trouble dealing with that. I don't feel pregnant."

"I didn't for a long time, either," Noelle said, "but I

wasn't talking about the baby. I meant there was going to be Carter."

"But he's not in my life."

"If you're going to have a baby together," Crissy told her, "then I would say he is. Permanently."

Chapter Five

Rachel paced nervously the last twenty minutes before Carter was due to arrive. Despite his promise for them to just "talk," she couldn't help remembering what had happened the last time he'd been here. Even worse, she couldn't seem to twist that remembering in such a way that she felt bad about it.

Okay, yes, the pregnancy had her totally freaked, and given the chance to magically undo the moment of conception, she was fairly sure she would. But she couldn't help breathing just a little faster every time she recalled what she'd felt like when he'd touched her. Which meant she would have to be extra careful tonight and make sure there wasn't a repeat of those events.

Things between them were complicated enough without adding that to the mix.

She glanced around at the dining alcove in her apartment. She'd set the table three different ways and had finally settled on the more casual place mats and paper napkins. This wasn't a date, after all. Just friends getting together to discuss some issues. Only she and Carter weren't friends and a baby counted for more than just an "issue."

She'd worked herself into such a frenzy that she was actually grateful when she heard footsteps on the balcony.

"Hi," she said, pulling open the front before he could knock.

"Hi, yourself." Carter smiled, then stepped inside. "I'd forgotten your thing for plants."

"It's a hobby," she admitted, motioning to the hanging baskets and overflowing tiered plant stands in the living room.

He handed her a picnic basket. "Dinner," he said. "I hope you like pasta."

"Sure. Who doesn't?"

He looked good. Normally she liked guys who were the more button-down-collar type, with short hair and loafers. Carter's shaggy dark blond hair hung nearly to his shoulders. He wore his faded red shirt outside his battered jeans and while he'd put on loafers, they were old and he wasn't wearing socks.

She should have been disapproving or at least unimpressed. Instead she found herself wanting to run her hands up and down his chest to see if the shirt was really as soft as it looked and he was as...

She hurried into the kitchen. Danger, she thought as she set the basket on the narrow counter. She had to keep her mind from wandering. She had to be smart and careful and...something else she couldn't remember right now.

She opened the basket and stared at the stacked glass containers inside. "What is all this?"

Carter moved close and peered over her shoulder. "Ravioli, extra sauce, salad, dressing, garlic bread and something for dessert. I can't tell what it is."

"You don't know what you made?"

He looked at her and grinned. "I didn't cook any of this. My sisters make regular contributions to my refrigerator. Word got out that we were having dinner together tonight and this appeared. I only dragged it along."

"Interesting system," she said, thinking it would be pretty nice to find dinner waiting for her when she got home after a long day.

"I like it. I never know what's for dinner, but then I enjoy surprises."

Even mine? Except she didn't ask the question—mostly because she wasn't sure she wanted to hear the answer.

"There are instructions," he said, reaching around her and pulling a piece of paper out of the basket.

She was aware of how close they were standing and the way his forearm almost brushed against her waist.

He handed her a typed sheet and for a second she

couldn't unclog her brain enough to read. Then she blinked and the words came into focus.

"Ravioli on the stove with the extra sauce," she said, telling herself it was a good thing that he moved back and refusing to feel disappointed that he hadn't spun her in his arms and kissed her. "Garlic bread in the oven. Salad and dressing in the refrigerator along with the dessert. Oh, it's tiramisu. Did one of your sisters really make it?"

"I guess."

"I've never had it homemade before. I can't wait."

"Merry will be delighted to know she's made a good impression."

He gave her a smile that made her insides quiver. Okay, she had to get a grip. She was reacting to his superficial good looks and some chemistry. But there were things that were much more important than that. Such as who Carter was as a man. She should focus on the insides and ignore the pretty package.

She put the food away, started the oven to preheat it, then asked if he'd like something to drink.

"I got a six-pack of that beer you were drinking at the bar," she said. "Would you like a bottle?"

"Sure. Thanks."

She collected it and a bottle of water for herself, then led the way back into her small living room. As they sat on the sofa, Rachel did her best to ignore the fact that these cushions had been the scene of the crime less than a month ago.

"Your sisters must live close to you," she said. "If they're bringing over food."

He leaned back and took a drink of his beer. "Too close. In a weak moment I bought a house on the same street as my mom and sisters. I like the free food delivery, but they're always dropping in, as you saw. I would like to be a little farther away, but right now moving would take too much time."

"Still, so much family nearby is nice."

He studied her with his dark eyes. "What happened to your family?"

She smoothed the front of her khakis. "My parents and my brother were killed in a car accident when I was twelve. There were no other relatives."

"I'm sorry," he said, leaning toward her. "What happened to you? Where did you go?"

"Into foster care." She shrugged. "Don't worry. It wasn't awful. The people who took me in were actually pretty nice. I grew up, finished high school and then went to college."

"You make it sound easy," he told her. "It can't have been. In one second, everything changed for you."

She still had nightmares about those days after the accident. About being all alone and knowing nothing would ever feel right again. She remembered vowing she would never, ever feel that much pain again and so far she'd managed to keep her word. She had friends, of course, but no one she couldn't imagine living without.

"It was hard," she admitted. "If I'd had grandparents or aunts or uncles, I think it would have been better. Some family to care about me."

"Now you take care of other people's children."

She smiled. "I know—it's not hard to figure out why I went into teaching. I wanted to be there for my kids."

"How long have you been teaching?"

People usually asked more questions about her loss. She sensed that Carter wanted more information and she appreciated his sensitivity in changing the subject. "This is my fourth year. I love everything about it. Even the messes. I asked the principal about starting a small garden in the spring and she okayed a nice open area near the play yard. That will be fun."

He glanced at the tangle of plants on the coffee table. "Just don't bring anything home. You're already at risk of becoming a pod person."

She laughed. "My plants know I love them. They'd never hurt me."

"You say that now, but wait until you wake up with a thorn growing out of your neck and stalks instead of arms."

"I'm not worried. What about you? Tell me about your work."

"I can't believe you're interested in carburetors and timing belts. You're too much a girl."

"Excuse me?" She raised her eyebrows. "Are you saying because of my gender, I'm not into cars?"

"Are you?"

"Well, no, but I could be if I wanted."

"Sure you could. So are you seeing anyone?"

The shift in subject startled her. "You mean like a guy?"

"I'm comfortable with your relationship with the plants."

She fought against the need to spring to her feet and glare down at him. "I wouldn't have slept with you if I'd been seeing someone else. How can you even ask? Are you seeing someone else?"

"I told you, I was off women until you came along and tempted me. It's not an unreasonable question."

"It is to me. I'm not that kind of person."

She regretted the words as soon as she spoke them. Gee, wow—talk about a moral code. She wasn't the kind of woman to sleep with one man while dating another, but she would bring a guy home from a bar and have sex with him.

"I've never done anything like that before," she murmured. "I shouldn't have…."

Carter slid across the sofa and touched her arm. "Hey, no beating yourself up. It's not allowed. Sometimes things happen and we deal with them. That's what we're doing right now. Dealing."

"But you think I'm awful."

"I don't. I think you got swept away, just like I did. Of course, I blame you for that."

She made a sound that was both a laugh and something way too close to a sob. No tears, she thought. Not over this. She preferred to save her crying for something more tragic. While she didn't know how she felt about being pregnant by a man she barely knew, no one had died. They would get through this.

"You okay?" he asked.

She nodded.

He moved back to his side of the sofa, which was

both good and bad. She liked having him close and touching her. Of course that would only lead to trouble.

"So we get to know each other," he said. "Then we make some decisions about how we're going to handle the baby."

"I agree." She picked up her bottle of water and looked at him. "You never proposed."

His reaction was almost comical. His whole body stiffened. His eyes darted from side to side and he looked ready to bolt.

"Did you want me to?"

She was impressed by how calm he sounded as he asked the question, and she did her best to hide her smile.

"It is traditional," she pointed out.

His gaze narrowed. "You're screwing with me."

She felt the corners of her mouth turn up. "Maybe a little."

He grinned. "I like that in a woman."

By the time they finished dinner, there was a whole lot more that he liked about Rachel. She was smart, and she was funny. She held her own when he pushed back and yet he could make her blush without trying.

"I would have expected lots of dance trophies all around the place," he said when they'd cleared the table and returned to the living room. "Didn't you say it was your secret passion?"

"It was. I had big plans to be a professional ballerina. If that didn't work out, I was willing to go be on Broadway."

"I'm sure New York theater was delighted to be your backup plan."

She laughed. "Yeah, I know. The arrogance of youth. Eventually I figured out I wasn't going to be a professional dancer, so I switched dreams."

There was something in the way she said the words that told him the decision hadn't been an easy one. "You kept on dancing, though."

"Sure. I take a couple of classes every week. More in the summer. I'm not sure how long I'll be able to keep them up." She touched her stomach as she spoke.

He eyed her belly and wondered when she would start showing. All his sisters had kids, but he'd never paid much attention to their pregnancies except to hope they had boys—which they never did.

"Any symptoms?" he asked.

"Aside from panic? Not yet. I'll be making a doctor's appointment to find out what I should and shouldn't be doing. I know to avoid alcohol and medications. Neither is really a problem for me. Aside from that, I'm in the dark."

"Me, too."

"You're a guy. That's expected. Shouldn't I have some maternal instincts that are activated just by me being pregnant?"

"Maybe they wait for the baby to be born."

She tucked her hair behind her ears. "I hope so, because otherwise, I'm pretty clueless."

"There's time."

"That's what I tell myself."

He looked around at the bright colors on the wall and the little touches like candles and bowls of stuff that smelled. "Your place is nice."

"Thanks. I like to decorate. Your house was nice, too. I only saw the living room, but it wasn't bachelor pad central."

"My sisters," he said by way of explanation. "They meddled."

She smiled. "In some cultures, that would be called helping."

"Yeah, well, in some cultures they'd ask first. But I didn't mind too much. They had some good ideas. I did most of the work myself. I remodeled the kitchen and did all the painting."

"Really? You know how to do that kind of thing?"

He nodded. "My mom worried about me growing up without a father and with only sisters in the house so she was always sending me off to spend the weekend with my friends and their dads. I learned to do basic carpentry, change oil in a car, ride a motorcycle. I don't think she was too excited about that last one."

"Not many mothers would be. But that was good of her, to take care of you that way."

"She's all right." He wasn't going to have a discussion about how much he loved his mother. That was too twisted for the already complicated situation. Time to get back to the one thing that had been on his mind since before dinner.

He leaned toward Rachel. He knew she'd been

kidding before, but he wasn't sure if she'd been hinting. "Did you want to get married, Rachel?"

Her eyes widened as she shook her head. "No. It's okay. No proposals are required. Really."

That was a relief. "So what do you want to do?"

She bit her lower lip, which probably meant she was confused. Most of him got that. But the real male part of him interpreted that little movement as an invitation. Sort of a "come kiss me" kind of invitation.

He wanted her. Even knowing she was pregnant didn't change that. He wanted to touch her and taste her and claim her. That single night together had been a good start, but there were so many things they hadn't done.

"What we're doing. Talking. Figuring it out without making any rash decisions."

"I can avoid rash," he said.

She smiled. "Have you ever been married?"

"No. Not my thing."

"Is it the fidelity issue? Being with just one woman?"

"I've only ever been with one woman at a time," he said. "Never cheated."

He'd never wanted to. It wasn't as if he needed *more* women in his life.

"You're not that into marriage, either," he said, remembering that she'd been engaged twice but never married.

"I will be," she told him. "It wasn't right before."

He almost asked what would make it right, because that's what he had trouble with. How did anyone know when it was right?

"Will you stay here?" he asked, nodding at the apartment.

"I haven't thought that far ahead. There are two bedrooms, but... Gee, now I have to think about moving. I guess the baby will want a yard."

"Not the first week."

She laughed. "Good point. I have time."

"If money's an issue, I could help."

She shifted on the sofa. "Okay, we've officially crossed into uncomfortable territory. Let's avoid talk of moving and money for a while."

"Fair enough."

She shook her head. "Carter, I'm really sorry this happened. I didn't mean to mess up your life. Or mine."

"We'll make it through. Kids aren't that bad."

"You don't actually know that."

"My sisters are doing fine and between them they have a bunch."

"So you're an uncle."

"Many times over. And now that they're married, there are finally guys around."

"There aren't *that* many women in your family."

He looked at her. "I only have nieces."

"You're kidding."

"No. Chances are you're having a girl."

She smiled. "I'd like that."

Under other circumstances, the relaxed body language and gentle smile would have been his cue to move in for a kiss and whatever else was being offered. Under these circumstances, that wouldn't be the wisest move.

Instead he stood and stretched. "I should get going. Thanks for dinner."

"I only heated it. I should thank you. And your sisters."

"I'll tell them you had seconds. That's thanks enough for them."

"Everything was great. Thanks for bringing it." She followed him to the front door. "We didn't really get anything resolved."

He smiled at her and fought against the need to feel her mouth on his. "Sure we did. I know you're a sucker for tiramisu and that dancing on Broadway was your second choice."

She swayed toward him. "You know what I mean. About the baby. But you're right. We have time. I…" She ducked her head, then looked at him. "I know neither of us wanted this to happen, but since it did, I'm glad it was you."

She blushed bright red. "I mean, you're really nice and I know you want me to think you're dangerous, but you're really not and I think you'll be a good dad. That's all I meant. Nothing, you know…"

"Mushy?"

She smiled. "Yeah. Mushy."

He gave in because after that little speech, how could he not? He put one hand on her shoulder, leaned toward her and lightly brushed her mouth with his.

Her lips were as warm and soft as he remembered. His body went on instant alert, but he ignored the wanting and drew back.

"I'll give you a call the first part of next week," he said. "We'll do this again."

"I'd like that. Night, Carter."

"Night."

He walked to his truck and climbed inside. It was barely ten on a Saturday night and he didn't feel like going home.

He made a U-turn and headed the couple of miles to the Blue Dog Bar. Once he arrived, he parked a street away and walked in through the kitchen entrance, so he wouldn't be seen by anyone up front.

George stood by the deep fryer where most of the snacks were made. "Hey, Carter. What's up?"

"Not much. Is Jenny around?"

"Sure. Watch this. They need to come out when the buzzer sounds. I'll go get her."

Carter monitored a basket of what looked like chicken wings until George returned with Jenny in tow.

"Hey, you," she said. "How are things?"

"Okay. Can you take a break?"

"Already told Dan I'd be gone for a few minutes."

Jenny followed him into a small breakroom in the back. At this hour it was empty. They settled on some plastic chairs placed around a round table.

"Dan was a little hurt," Jenny said. "You know he hates it when you talk to me instead of him."

"He's a typical guy, same as me. How is he going to help?"

"He's not," Jenny said with a grin. "But he has delusions of grandeur."

"Is that why you married him?"

"I couldn't wait for you forever, darlin'."

"I don't remember you waiting at all." He leaned back in the chair. "You called my mother."

"I know. I was there."

"You're supposed to be *my* friend. That means being on my side."

"There's a baby now, Carter. You don't get a side."

"Still, you could have waited."

"Actually I called more for Rachel than for you."

He didn't question how Jenny knew Rachel's name. Her sisters were close to Jenny and would have filled her in on everything they knew.

"Rachel's fine."

"I wanted to be sure," Jenny said. "I have to tell you, I'm surprised. You were always compulsively careful."

There was something about the way she said it. "Was that a problem for you?"

"Not a problem, more of a symptom. You made it clear you wouldn't be trapped and while I wasn't interested in that, a woman likes to think a man can be swept away from time to time."

"Look what happens when he is."

Jenny nodded. "You don't seem too angry."

"I'm not. I'm…" He wasn't sure what he felt. He'd always liked kids and had thought he'd want them in his life. It was the whole marriage thing he couldn't relate to.

"Think I have what it takes to be a good father?" he asked lightly, although he was deadly serious about the question.

"Absolutely," she said. "You'll be great. You know your mom thinks you should marry Rachel."

"I think she mentioned that. What do you think?"

"That a baby changes everything. For what it's worth, marriage is pretty cool."

"I can't believe you're happy with Dan when you had me."

She laughed. "He loves me and you never did. Besides, you're not all that."

"Sure I am."

"Okay, yes you are, but you were never the one for me and I wasn't the one for you."

He didn't think he had a "one" but there was no point in saying that to Jenny.

She stood, walked around the table, then bent over and kissed him on the cheek. "You're going to be a daddy, Carter. It's time to stop playing and grow up."

"I'm plenty grown-up."

"You're still fooling around. Look at what you're doing with your life. Get a real job."

He frowned. "I have a real job."

"You know what I mean." She touched his earring. "You've always gotten by on charm and looks, that body and a great personality. Now it's time for some substance."

"Ouch."

"I only say this because I love you. I have to get back to work."

She left the breakroom. Carter stayed where he was.

Jenny had always been able to say the words. For her,

professing love was as easy as folding socks. But not for him. Oh, he knew he loved his family and cared about his friends. But love, romantic love?

Not even once.

He told himself it didn't matter. That he was still a great guy. He almost believed it, too. Only he couldn't figure out why his heart had never been touched and what about him would change if it was.

Rachel picked up the containers of paint and carried them to the sink. The mess was indescribable, but it had been worth it. Her class had met all its goals for the week and because of that, they'd been able to pick their reward. Unfortunately for her, the reward had been finger painting. Both she and the room were now brightly colored and smudgy, but the water-based product would wash off and she and her class had had a great time together. She'd even created a finger-painting masterpiece of her own, although she had no idea what she was going to do with it.

She'd just finished washing off the tables when she noticed three men walking toward her classroom. They'd come through the play area, so they were visible through the large set of windows in her room. All three were in uniform, two from the local police and one in what looked like a firefighter uniform.

Her first thought was that they were coming to arrest her, only she hadn't done anything wrong. Her second was that her apartment had burned down. She met them at the door.

"Is it bad?" she asked fearfully. "Is everything gone?"

The firefighter smiled. "Everything's fine. You're Rachel Harper, right?"

Everything was all right? "Yes, that's me."

"Good," one of the cops said. "We'd hate to welcome the wrong person into the family."

Rachel blinked. "Excuse me?"

One of the guys nudged the other two. "This works better if we introduce ourselves. I'm Frank and I'm married to Liz. This is Adam. He's with Merry." He pointed to the other police officer. "Gordon's married to Shelly. This is complicated enough without worrying about last names. You can learn them later."

It took her a second to figure out what they were talking about. "You're married to Carter's sisters," she said more to herself than to them.

Gordon, the firefighter, said, "The family is kind of crazy close, but that's what makes them so special. Our wives have been talking about you, so we thought we'd come down and introduce ourselves when things were quiet. It will make it easier to get to know the family."

"It was really nice of you to stop by," she said, "and I don't mean to sound rude, but why did you?"

"Because of Carter. Now that the two of you are getting married," Frank said.

"Married?" Rachel took a step back. "I don't think so. Not married. Carter and I barely…" She hesitated, thinking that due to her pregnancy, saying she and Carter barely knew each would be really tacky. She cleared her throat. "We're not getting married."

All three men glanced at her midsection. "You have to," Gordon said. "You're going to have Carter's baby."

That was the theory, she thought, still not sure any of this was real, although thinking about it too much sent her into a panic.

"Once you start to show," Adam said, "won't you want to be married? I know this is sudden, but Carter's a good guy to have at your back. I'd trust him with my life. I have."

She frowned. "Excuse me? How? He works in a motorcycle shop."

"Right." Adam shrugged. "Still, I'd let him date my sister."

There was a recommendation, Rachel thought, not sure if she should laugh or run for the hills.

"You're all being terrific," she said carefully. "I really appreciate the support and the welcome, but Carter and I…"

Three pairs of disapproving eyes focused on her.

"That is, I don't think we…" She pressed her lips together. This was her life. She didn't have to answer to anyone. If Carter was happy to not marry her, why did these guys get a vote?

But she didn't know how to say that and for reasons not clear to her, she couldn't seem to tell the three of them to mind their own business. Maybe it was because they were part of a family and she'd wanted that ever since she'd lost hers.

"We're dating," she said at last, doing her best not to wince at the lie. "We're dating and we're really hopeful."

She smiled brightly and prayed that was enough. The three guys nodded.

"Good," Frank said. "Okay, then. We'll let you get back to work now. But if you need anything—I mean anything—just call. One of us can always get to you. Okay? You're not alone anymore, Rachel. You're one of us."

With that, they left. She stared after them knowing that the smart, independent side of her should resent the implication that she couldn't handle things on her own. When in truth, she was really touched by their visit and envious of their closeness. What would it be like to be a part of a family like that?

She drew in a deep breath and reminded herself that she had a more pressing problem. Namely informing Carter that they were now a dating couple. Honestly, she had no idea how he was going to take the news.

Chapter Six

Carter arrived at Rachel's house after work. She'd left a message for him on his cell, saying that his brothers-in-law had stopped by and that she needed to talk to him. She hadn't said much else, but then she hadn't had to. He could imagine how the conversation had gone.

As he climbed up the stairs to her apartment, he wondered if any of the three had told her about his real job. Some women were fine with it but others freaked.

She opened the door before he could knock. "Thanks for coming. I just didn't…" She drew in a breath. "Okay. Come in and we'll talk, right? Because that's what rational grown-ups do. We talk. We don't panic, we don't allow ourselves to be influenced by the thoughts of others. Especially people we don't know. I mean, I'm sure your family is perfectly lovely, but they don't have the right to dictate how I live my life. Plus, I have to say, I hated the disapproval. I understand it, sort of. They care about you and they want you to get what you want. I don't mind that, either, but you've made it really clear you're not interested in marrying me and who am I to complain? I don't want to get married, either."

He'd been content to let her wind down, but when it became obvious that wasn't going to happen anytime soon, he stepped in to fix the problem.

He moved into the apartment, grabbed Rachel by her upper arms, drew her to him and kissed her firmly on the mouth.

He had a brief impression of heat and softness, then he pulled back. The reaction was exactly what he'd hoped. She stopped talking and stared at him.

"You kissed me."

"I know," he said with a grin. "I was there."

"I didn't think there would be kissing."

"There doesn't have to be if you don't like it. I didn't know how else to get you to take a breath. Whatever happened, we can fix it."

She closed the front door behind him and shook her head. "You'd think so, wouldn't you? But I have my doubts."

He had a feeling she was going to get wound up again, and while he wouldn't mind the excuse to kiss her a second time, they needed to make a little progress on the information front.

"Tell me what happened," he said as he led her to the brightly colored sofa and urged her to sit. "Start at the beginning."

She sank down. He settled next to her and waited.

"Your brothers-in-law came to visit me at school today."

He groaned. "During class?"

"No, after." She flopped against the back of the sofa. "How on earth would I have explained them if they'd showed up in the middle of the day? Five-year-olds can ask a lot of questions. I can only imagine the phone calls from worried parents after a visit like that."

"There won't be another visit like that," he told her, knowing when he got home, he was going to have a little talk with his sisters. He appreciated their concern, but this wasn't their business.

"I hope you're right," Rachel told him. "I mean it was really nice to meet them, even if I wasn't sure who was who, let alone which guy had which sister. But Carter, they think we're getting married. They sort of implied it was required. I don't know what I want. I haven't even accepted the fact that I'm pregnant. I saw the truth on the test sticks, so I have the information in my head, but I really don't believe it. Not yet. And when I do try to convince myself that it's real, I start to hyperventilate, and that can't be good."

She was adorable, he thought as he watched her sit up and give a good imitation of someone unable to catch her breath.

"Relax," he told her. "Take a deep breath and hold it."

She did as he suggested.

"Now let it out."

She exhaled.

"You're fine," he said, wishing he had another excuse to kiss her or even touch her soft wavy curls. Her hair was a tempting combination of reds and browns and gold. He remembered how it had felt in his fingers the one night they'd made love. Of course touching her hair was only one of several experiences he would like to repeat.

"I don't feel fine," she admitted. "I feel weird. I don't want to disappoint your family. I know they're important to you. But I won't be dictated to."

"No one's dictating."

"It felt like that."

"That doesn't make it real. This is between the two of us. We'll work it out in the best way for us."

She ducked her head. "It's not that simple," she whispered. "There were three of them and I felt trapped."

He could imagine. "What did you say?"

She looked at him. "That we were dating and hoping for the best."

He could live with that. Besides, she looked so dejected and guilty that he couldn't be annoyed with her. "So you didn't promise to marry me."

"Of course not." She narrowed her gaze. "Are you smiling? This is *not* funny."

He kept his expression as neutral as he could make it. "I'm not smiling."

"It looks like you are. Nothing about this is funny.

We're talking about lives on the line here. We've made a baby. When I think about that, I can't breathe anymore. Besides, this is all your fault."

"Hey, how do you figure? There were two of us doing the wild thing that night."

"Exactly. But if you hadn't kissed me like that, I wouldn't have given in."

He'd been about to get defensive, but now there was no need. "My kissing won you over, huh?"

She shifted away from him. "Don't take that as a compliment. I didn't mean it that way."

"Right. Being a good kisser is a bad thing."

"It is when it gets two strangers in trouble," she muttered. "Don't you dare get smug on me. I couldn't stand it."

He was feeling a lot of things, but smug wasn't one of them. Right now what he wanted most was a chance to kiss her again and cause her to lose control. Not his most sensible plan, he admitted, but a guy could dream.

"Besides," she continued, "our more pressing problem is your family. You know those guys are going to talk to your sisters and then what? They'll tell your mom and everyone will think we're dating."

And that statement was the answer, he thought suddenly. "Dating isn't a bad idea."

She stared at him. "Excuse me? How is that going to help?"

"We can use this. Dating would be the next logical step, under the circumstances. If we were serious about working on a relationship, I mean. So we date. Or tell my family we're dating. We can even act like we're dating. Then, in a couple of months, we'll tell everyone things didn't work out. Relationships fail all the time. The family will think we really tried and get off our backs and we'll be free to work out things as we want to."

She tilted her head. "I like it," she said slowly. "You'll be okay with your family and they won't think I'm awful."

"They don't think that now."

"You didn't see the looks on those guys' faces," she told him.

Carter felt his fingers curl into his palms. He had been delighted when his sisters had gotten married. The more guys in the family, the better, as far as he was concerned. But knowing they'd made Rachel uncomfortable had him thinking about pounding each one of them into a bloody pulp.

"Okay, we're pretend dating," she said. "We'll need some sort of plan and schedule. You won't be able to see anyone else while this is going on. It wouldn't look right."

"Not a problem," he told her, consciously letting go of his anger. "I'm swearing off women again."

"Are you sure you want to do that?" she asked, her voice teasing. "Look at what happened the last time."

"Not my fault. You were too tempting to resist."

She leaned back and laughed. "Oh, please. Me?"

"Yes, you. Don't you consider yourself a temptation?"

The smile lingered, bringing light to her green eyes. "Not even on my best day, but it's sweet of you to say so. Now about your job."

The quick change in topic didn't give him much time to brace himself. Had they told her the truth or not?

"Want to see a pay stub?" he asked.

"Not especially. But why did Frank and the others act so strange when I reminded them you worked in a motorcycle shop? You're not on probation, are you?"

He chuckled and held up his right hand. Good news—they hadn't told her. "I swear I have never been arrested, convicted or incarcerated. Ever."

"That's encouraging. They're all cops and firefighters. Don't they approve of what you do?"

"I…"

He found himself not wanting to lie to her. She was going to have to know eventually and if she reacted badly, better now than later.

There were rules about who could know and mothers of unborn children fell in the "yes" category. But it was more than just that. There was the woman herself and how carefully she would protect the information.

"What are you thinking?" she asked. "Should I be scared?"

"No. But I will need you to give your word that you won't tell anyone what I'm going to tell you."

"Or you'll have to shoot me?" she asked. "What are we talking about? I can't figure out if I should laugh or make a run for my car."

"I'm a cop working undercover. This job at the motorcycle shop is part of my cover. I'm working on a case involving counterfeit parts brought into this country from overseas."

She blinked. "You're a…"

"Police officer."

"But your hair is so long."

He laughed then and, without thinking, pulled her close. "Damn, Rachel, you're never boring."

She held herself stiffly for a second before relaxing into his embrace. "You haven't known me long enough to be bored," she murmured. "That could come later."

"I don't think so."

His body reacted to her nearness with a predictable rush of blood and need. But he kept the embrace light. They weren't going to do that again, remember?

He released her and straightened. She studied him.

"They know about the earring?" she asked.

He grinned. "It's all part of the assignment. I have a gun and a badge if you want to see them."

"No, thanks. I believe you. So that's why your brothers-in-law acted so strange. They were surprised I didn't know the truth."

He shrugged. "Probably."

"Your mom can't like what you do. She must worry all the time."

"She's used to it. I come from a long line of cops. My grandfather, my great-grandfather. My dad was one. He died before I was born."

She winced. "I'm sorry. Was it work-related?"

He nodded. "A drunk driver got him while he was on patrol."

"Oh, Carter. That must have been so awful for your

mom and your sisters. And for you, growing up without a dad."

"I appreciate the sympathy," he said, "but it's not necessary. I don't know any different."

"Everything is so complicated," she said. "How did that happen?"

"We made a baby."

Her eyes widened slightly. "I'm still not comfortable thinking about that. Could we avoid the topic?"

"Not for much longer."

"I know, but we have a plan, right? Pretend dating." She grinned. "Does that mean you bring me plastic flowers instead of real ones?"

"Would you like that?"

She glanced around the apartment. "I have plenty of real ones, so I'm good."

He started to ask what she would like instead, but stopped himself. Pretend dating meant putting on a show, not getting involved in any way. They could be friends, but nothing more.

Friends who sleep together, he thought hopefully, and then reminded himself he'd sworn off women again. He had to. Look at what had happened with Rachel.

Women were the root of all the trouble in his life and he would be better off if he could simply walk away from them.

Then Rachel smiled and he found himself wanting her again. Okay, so he would swear off women *after* they worked this pretend dating thing out. Maybe they could figure out a way to have pretend sex. That could be fun.

* * *

Rachel smoothed the foil on top of the casserole she carried. "I hope this is okay. I didn't know what to make. I don't cook a lot but my seven-layer bean dip is really popular at all the teacher potlucks at school. Of course, free food is rarely criticized, so maybe that's not a good standard. Should I have made something else? An entrée? Or dessert? Is bean dip enough?"

Carter pulled his front door shut and stared at her. "You do that a lot, don't you."

Rachel found herself momentarily caught up in his brown eyes and the little crinkly lines that formed when he smiled, like now. She had to shake her head to clear her brain.

"I'm sorry, what was the question?"

He chuckled and took the casserole dish from her. "You get wound up when you're nervous. I like it. Of course the best way to get you back on earth seems to be to kiss you and we both know that's not a good idea, so we're going to need another plan."

She wasn't so sure. Carter's kisses tended to totally clear her mind and as nervous as she felt right now, she wouldn't mind forgetting the reason.

"We're walking?" she asked as they moved past his truck and her car.

"No point in driving." He paused and pointed across the street and down one house. "That's where Mama lives. Merry is next to her. Liz and Shelly live in the other direction. Three houses down and that one on the corner."

"That's really close," she said, surprised he would plant himself in the middle of all that family.

He sighed as they crossed the street. "Yeah, I know," he muttered. "I wasn't thinking when I bought this place. It's too close. One of these days I'm going to move."

"Still, you enjoy your family and that's nice." She could appreciate the need to stay connected. If her parents and brother were still alive...

She pushed the thought away. Not going there right now. She was nervous enough without adding a little heartache to the mix.

She distracted herself by remembering how great Carter had been about the dating issue. He could have gotten upset, but he hadn't, which made him a good guy in her eyes. Of course he'd already proved himself a good guy by how he'd reacted to her pregnancy. Now that she thought about it, she'd pretty much been one disaster after the other where he was concerned.

They reached the front door of his mother's house. Carter walked in without knocking and yelled, "We're here."

Rachel could hear voices coming from the back of the house, then Nina Brockett hurried out to greet them.

"Late as always. Some mothers would take that as a message. Some mothers would think their only son was trying to say he was no longer interested in visiting his old mother."

"Some mothers are just a little too dramatic for their own good," he said, bending down and kissing her on the cheek. "You remember Rachel."

His mother, an attractive, petite woman smiled broadly at Rachel, then held out both her arms. "Of course. Welcome, welcome."

Rachel found herself hugged, then kissed on the cheek. "Thanks for having me, Mrs. Brockett."

"Nina. I insist." She nudged Carter with her elbow. "We'll have her calling me Mama like everyone else before too long, eh? So what's this? You made something. See? A girl who can cook. That's new for you. A step up. Come, come. We're all in the kitchen. No matter how nice I make the rest of the house, everyone wants to be in the kitchen."

"It's Carter and Rachel," Nina called as she led the way into the overly crowded kitchen. "Carter, remind her who everyone is. Oh, what's this, dear?" She took the casserole dish from Carter.

"A seven-layer dip," Rachel said. "Carter mentioned you always had chips on hand."

"You didn't have to bring anything, but I appreciate that you did. Very thoughtful. Carter, she's thoughtful. Did you notice?"

Rachel felt herself blush but before she could say anything, she was caught up in another confusing round of introductions.

There were too many people in the small space. Adults, kids, a large dog.

Carter pointed to his sisters. "Merry, Liz and Shelly," he said. "Their husbands are Adam, Frank and Gordon."

She recognized the three men who had visited her the previous week, although now that they were in casual clothes instead of their uniforms, she wasn't sure who was who. As for Carter's sisters, she was pretty sure that Merry had short dark hair and Shelly had long brown hair, but if anyone got a haircut, she was in trouble for sure.

"And you remember Jenny, from the Blue Dog Bar, right?" Carter asked.

Jenny?

Rachel turned and found herself staring into the smiling face of the pretty female bartender.

"Hi," Jenny said. "Good to see you again."

"Hello."

Rachel opened her mouth and closed it. She didn't know how to politely ask what the woman was doing here. Staying in touch was one thing, but like this?

"I'm an ex-girlfriend," Jenny said, obviously reading Rachel's confusion. "Carter and I dated for a while about…what, five years ago, I guess."

Carter put his arm around Rachel's shoulder. "We broke up, but would she go away? Not even for money."

Jenny lightly punched him in the arm. "You *never* offered to pay me to leave. I might have left then." She smiled at Rachel. "Carter's a great guy, but he does seem to hang on to his women. Even when he dumps us."

Rachel didn't know what to think. She'd never been in a situation like this, and she wasn't sure what she should say or do.

"You dumped me," Carter said. "I'm sure of it."

"Sorry, no," Jenny said with a smile. "But don't sweat it. I'm grateful." She turned back to Rachel. "Carter broke my heart, so I decided to date someone totally inappropriate. It turns out, Dan was the love of my life." She held up her left hand and wiggled her ring finger. The diamond band there sparkled impressively. "We've been married three years now."

Just then a little girl burst into the kitchen. "Tanya stole the ball and she won't let me play." After her announcement, she burst into tears.

"I'll handle this," Merry said. She picked up the child and carried her back outside. Jenny excused herself and went with her.

Rachel found herself being offered a drink—she chose flavored water—and a chair, which she declined. A few minutes later, in a relatively private moment, she turned to Carter.

"You and Jenny really went out?" she asked.

He shrugged. "Yeah. But it was a long time ago. It doesn't mean anything."

"I don't mean to be rude or too curious, but why is she here?"

"Sometimes my mom and sisters like one of my girlfriends enough to keep her around even after we stop going out. It's made for some entertaining holidays, I can tell you."

"You mean several of them will join in with the family?"

"Sure. It's okay if they bring a date, but when they're single, it's a little uncomfortable. Or they become close friends. I dated this other woman, Shawna. She and Jenny got so close they were in each other's weddings."

She was torn between wanting to get the facts and wondering if she'd crossed the line into the land of too much information.

"I'm not sure this is a completely normal family," she murmured.

He leaned close enough for her to feel his breath on her ear. "I can tell you that it's not, but that's what makes it so much fun."

She was aware of every part of his body. The need to lean in—to touch and be touched—was powerful and just a little scary.

"So, how are you two getting along?"

Rachel jumped as Nina appeared from nowhere with a plate of tiny quiches.

"We're good," Carter said as he took three quiches, placed them on a napkin and handed them to Rachel. "How about you? Having fun?"

His mother ignored the question. "A baby changes everything. Have you thought of that? It's not just you anymore. There's another life."

Rachel was glad she hadn't taken a bite. She had a bad feeling that she would have choked.

"You're kidding," Carter said as he collected a couple of quiches for himself. "Another life. Huh. I didn't know that. I just thought, 'Hey, a baby. We'll keep it on the bookcase.'"

His mother glared at him. "I'm being serious."

"You're meddling," he said. "We talked about that."

His mother turned to Rachel. "You're a sensible girl. What do your parents say about all this?"

Rachel opened her mouth, then closed it. She cleared her throat. "My parents are gone. They died in a car accident when I was twelve. My baby brother was with them and he was killed as well."

She felt Carter's gaze on her. Nina touched her arm. "So it's just you? You have no other relatives?"

Rachel managed a smile. "I'm okay."

"Of course you are," the older woman said. "You have us, now. We're your family. We'll be there for you. No matter what. You have a problem, you call. Promise?"

Rachel felt a tightness in her throat. "Thank you."

Nina smiled and moved away.

"She's trying to be supportive," Carter said when they were alone.

"I know. She wants me to feel welcome. Better that than stoning me or something."

"We gave up stoning awhile ago."

"Good to know."

"Mama's a little over-the-top," he said. "But she's right. You do have all of us now."

"Wherever will I put you?" she asked, her voice deliberately teasing. There was already so much going on today, she didn't need an emotional moment to push her over the edge.

Just then one of Carter's sisters walked over. Rachel was pretty sure it was Liz.

"I'm glad you two agreed to get married," she said. "Mama is so excited. She was starting to think no one would ever trap Carter."

Rachel winced. "I didn't exactly trap him."

"Sure you did, but don't worry about it. He's had it coming for years."

Carter sighed. "Thanks for the support, sis."

"No problem. I've always taken care of my baby brother. Oh, Tanya, honey, no. That's breakable. You put that down right now."

Liz fled across the room.

"You didn't trap me," Carter said in a low voice. "We're in this together, making our own decisions."

Rachel nodded, but inside she felt funny. She'd never thought of herself as the kind of woman who would have to trap a man into being involved with her. And she hadn't. As he'd said, she and Carter were figuring out what they wanted for themselves. They weren't a couple. This wasn't even a real date. So why did she feel guilty?

"Do you want this baby?" she asked.

"Absolutely," he said without hesitating. "I might have issues with women, but all my life I've wanted to be a father. I don't know anything about it, but I'm willing to learn. I want to be there for my kid. I want to make a difference in her life."

She smiled. "Still convinced we're having a girl?"

"It's just my luck."

"What about my luck?" she asked.

He grinned. "You have me. How much luckier could you get?"

It was dark when Rachel and Carter walked back to his house. She felt tired, but in a good way. There were still complications to be dealt with, and she doubted she would ever figure out who was who in his family, but she'd felt welcomed with open arms.

"I like them," she said as he opened his front door and let Goldie push into the house first. "Everyone was great."

He sighed heavily. "I knew it. This always happens. A guy thinks he's getting lucky because he's charming or smart and then he finds out that the only thing his girl is interested in is his family."

He was teasing, of course, but even more intriguing was his use of the words *his girl*. She wasn't. That wasn't the deal. But for a moment, she felt a shiver of something very close to longing.

"I find it hard to believe you've ever had trouble getting women on your own," she said. "So don't look for sympathy here."

"Ouch. After my family *and* heartless. I'm crushed."

He looked good crushed, she thought, studying the strong, handsome lines of his face before finding her interest settling on his mouth. Carter had a lot of good qualities but right at the top was his amazing ability to kiss her until her entire body turned to mush.

"You'll survive," she murmured, knowing she should look away but finding it difficult to do so. Just one little kiss. What could it hurt?

"Rachel."

He spoke her name in a low growl that caused goose bumps to break out on her arms and the little hairs on the back of her neck to prickle.

She forced herself to take a step back. Right. Be sensible. "Complications," she said as she reached for her car keys in her purse's outside pocket. "We don't need any more complications. There are other things we need to deal with." Although at the moment, she couldn't remember what they were.

"Don't look at me like that," he told her.

"Like what?"

"Like you mean it."

Before she could decide if she did or not, he leaned in and kissed her. As it was exactly what she'd been hoping for, she did little more than melt against him and wish she could purr.

His arms came around her, supporting her, comforting and arousing. She felt his strong hands on her back. Her purse slipped to the ground, but she managed to keep hold of her car keys. That was something, right? That meant she wasn't totally losing control.

But it was hard to stay sane when he moved his lips against hers in a way designed to make her go crazy. She couldn't figure out if it was the pressure, the intensity or some chemical connection that defied description. Whatever the cause, she wanted him right then. The fact that they were still on his front porch didn't matter.

She parted for him. He nipped her lower lip before slipping his tongue inside.

The first erotic stroke made her thighs tremble. The second had her insides clenching and the third had her wet and swollen and nearly whimpering with need.

He moved his hands up and down her back. She wanted to grab his wrists and guide him so that his clever fingers could touch her breasts. She wanted to be swept away by the most intense passion she'd ever experienced. She wanted…

He drew back.

Every cell in her body screamed in protest as he stepped away and gave her a regretful smile.

"Not a good idea," he said.

Of course it wasn't a good idea. But wasn't that the point? How could he be rational at a time like this?

Still, she wouldn't let him know that she hadn't wanted him to stop.

"I'll be going," she said, proud of herself to being able to speak in a steady, nearly normal tone of voice. "Have a nice evening."

"You, too."

A few deep breaths helped clear her mind enough for her to remember their plan. Pretend dating only. Nothing more. A smart woman would quit while she was ahead and Rachel had always been one of the brightest girls in her class.

Chapter Seven

"You don't have to do this," Carter said, sounding more apprehensive than he should have.

Rachel held in a grin as she slipped her hand into the crook of his arm and sighed. "I *want* to do this. You did a beautiful job remodeling your kitchen. Now it's time to finish it off."

"It *is* finished," he grumbled as they walked through the aisles of the large home-improvement store.

"White walls? Come on. Have a little imagination. Color is our friend. Besides, you get to pick any color you want. You don't have to run it by your landlord and then plead for your choice."

"My choice is white."

She chuckled. "No, it's not. Besides, it's too stark

against the maple cabinets. Quite the bold selection here in Southern California, where most people favor oak."

He shrugged. "I thought they looked nice."

"They do. They're beautiful and they deserve something better than white walls."

He mumbled something under his breath, but Rachel didn't mind. If Carter really had wanted to keep those stark white walls, he wouldn't have asked her to come with him after work to look at paint chips.

The invitation might fall under the category of "pretend dating" but she intended to enjoy every minute of it.

"You're lucky to have your own house," she said. "I'm saving, but with real estate prices what they are, it's going to take me awhile. But I have a whole shoe box full of articles and pictures I've cut out of magazines, or downloaded off Web sites. I have this dream about the perfect closet, all organized with shoe shelves and hooks for belts and purses."

He eyed her suspiciously. "We're just here for paint."

"I know that. Don't worry. I don't expect you to completely redo your closets just to satisfy my urges. At least not this week."

He groaned and she laughed.

They walked into the paint department. Carter held out the small drawer she'd insisted they bring along to help with the color choices.

"So maybe cream?" he said. "Cream would look nice with the maple."

"I don't think so." She ignored the chips of cream

and white and headed to the yellows. "Nothing super-bright," she murmured more to herself than him. "It has to blend. But nothing too boring."

Carter had gone with black appliances, which made it easy, and a fairly neutral black, gray and cream flecked granite. The cabinets were light, and that meant a bland paint color would cause the whole room to fade away.

"A warm color," she said. "You get that great morning sun in there."

She plucked out three different yellows, then moved to peach. "Hmm, more on the orange side or more salmon?"

Carter took a step back. "That's a lot of color."

"I know. We'll grab all the ones that interest us, then narrow the choice down to three or four. Then we buy samples. Better to paint big squares of color on the wall and live with it for a week, than get the wrong color."

She fanned out her selections. Rather than pick, he made a strangled sound in his throat.

"Are you always like this?" she asked. "It's paint, not a room full of snakes."

"I could deal with snakes."

"What a typical guy."

"That's me. Mr. Beige."

She discarded a couple of samples until they had four she liked and he didn't flinch at. After collecting the samples, she dragged him over to the fabric department.

He stared at the bolts of cloth. "Why are we here?"

"I was thinking I could make some valances for your windows. Nothing fancy, but they'd dress them up."

He looked as if he was about to run for cover. "Those go on the top of the window, right?"

"Uh-huh. The miniblinds are practical, but not especially attractive. Roman shades would be nice, but I can't see you agreeing to that, what with how you've reacted to a little color."

He stiffened. "I'm reacting fine. I have samples here. I'm going to put them on the wall."

"I know, but you're pretty whiny about it."

He looked outraged. "I do not whine."

"Of course not."

"I am rational and completely in control of the situation."

She held in a smile. "Okay, so I was thinking of something like this."

She pulled out a bolt of fabric and spread out the cloth, then put the paint chips on top. "See how they all go."

He frowned. "How did you do that? You just picked that one out and it's perfect? That's not right."

"I'm gifted. Now, do you like this?"

He studied the striped fabric. "Yeah. There aren't any flowers on it."

"You're not the flower type. So we'll get the fabric, then when you choose the paint color, we'll use the valance material to pick out coordinating chair mats and a tablecloth for that little table. The simple stripe in the valance means you can get a different pattern for those or none at all."

He nodded slowly. "My sisters talk like that, too. Is it a chick thing?"

"Yes. Most of us are born with the ability to coordinate fabric."

He rubbed the cloth. "It's nice. I like it better than white."

"It's a miracle."

"Carter?"

The woman's voice came from behind them. Rachel turned and saw a pretty, petite redhead holding a bolt of fabric.

"Hi, Nora," Carter said. "How are you?"

"Okay."

"Good. Rachel, this is Nora."

The other woman nodded. "Hi. Nice to meet you. So you're with Carter now, huh? We used to go out." The hunger in her expression said she would like to again. "You look…great."

"You, too," he said as he gently put his hand on Rachel's shoulder.

Rachel felt both awkward and uncomfortable. Should she excuse herself so Carter and Nora could speak in private? Good manners dictated that she at least offer, but she couldn't seem to form the words or make her feet move.

Nora cleared her throat. "I thought maybe, you know, sometime we could go out for coffee."

"Thanks, but this isn't a good time for me. You take care, Nora."

"Yeah. Okay. Well, bye."

She shuffled off.

Carter watched her go, then shook his head. "Sorry about that."

"It's fine. I take it you two had a bad breakup?"

"Yeah. Usually I can stay friends, but Nora wanted marriage or nothing."

"You weren't interested in her that way?"

Carter looked at her. "I'm not interested in anyone that way. All my life I've been told I'll meet someone, fall in love and get married. So far, it hasn't happened. I love women—all women. I don't cheat, I'm more interested in quality than volume, but forever? Not my style. I don't need to grow old with anyone."

As he spoke his expression tightened.

"What?" she asked. "Do you expect me to get mad?"

He shrugged. "I'm braced for the criticism. Most women don't appreciate my position."

"I do," she told him and meant it. "Why marry someone you don't love?" She drew in a breath. "That's what happened to me with my two engagements. I thought I loved the guys, but as time passed, I realized I didn't. I started to feel trapped. Neither of them understood."

He relaxed a little. "So what do you think of marriage?"

She thought of what she remembered of her parents' relationship. "I think with the right person, it can be the best part of anyone's life. I want that, but only when it's right. And it needs to be for the right reasons."

"I won't ever want to get married."

She smiled. "I'm okay with that, Carter. I don't plan to be one of your groupies."

"I don't have groupies."

"Oh, you're wrong, but that's okay. I can totally respect not wanting to make a commitment to someone you don't love. What I don't understand is not making a commitment to one of these beautiful paints. Now *that* would break my heart."

He grinned. "Fine. I'll put the damn paint on the damn wall and pick one."

"You promise?"

"Yes."

"Good. I'll make valances."

"You can't."

"Actually, I'm pretty good with my old, trusty sewing machine. I learned while I was still dancing. Costumes cost too much to buy. None of my foster families could afford it, so I learned to sew."

"I don't mean that. I'll owe you."

"And that's bad why?"

"I don't know how to pay you back."

Images of them naked and touching and joining instantly filled her brain. Okay, she could give him a list of ways to pay her back, starting with a few long, slow, deep kisses, followed by some serious naked time.

Without meaning to, she remembered how his hands had felt on her body. How he touched her with an irresistible combination of aggressive tenderness that had left her weak and hungry for more. He could...

"Earth to Rachel."

"What? Oh." She blinked at him. "Sorry. What was the question?"

"If you're going to do this for me, I want to do something for you. What do you need? Heavy furniture moved? A tree planted in your honor?"

She laughed. "Nothing like that. But I do have the fall festival coming up at school. Each class has to build a booth. Now that I've seen your handiwork, I think maybe you're the right one to take on the job of being in charge."

"Done."

"Are you sure? We're talking about ten five-year-olds and some fairly inept parents."

"I like kids, and parents find me very charming."

"Especially the moms."

He flashed her a smile. "Especially."

Carter tucked his too-long hair under a baseball cap and then turned up the collar of his jacket. The truck stop diner was several miles north of Riverside on I-15. As this was the main drag to Las Vegas, there were plenty of people coming and going. A good place for a private meeting.

He'd already seen his captain's car in the parking lot, so he walked in and looked for the table.

Captain Don Killian was known for protecting his men, so Carter wasn't surprised to see the older man at a booth in the back. Carter slid in across from him and realized a large pole would conceal him from view.

"Nicely done," he said with a grin.

Killian shrugged. "I had to wait for an old couple to

clear out, but I figured this was the best seat in the house. How's it going, Carter?"

"Good."

The waitress appeared. Both men ordered burgers and sodas. When she left, Carter leaned forward.

"There's going to be a big shipment out next week. I've got a copy of the parts inventory heading out. The drop is in Chicago, and from there it goes all across the country."

Carter was part of a team investigating counterfeit auto parts brought in from other countries.

While Carter went over the details, Killian wrote down the information.

"We can intercept this," his captain said. "I'll talk to the Feds on the case, but the current plan is we'll make it look like a highway accident so no one gets suspicious. We're thinking maybe four or five more weeks on the job. You okay with that?"

The waitress arrived with their drinks. Carter waited until she'd left before saying, "Sure. I'm good. No one suspects anything."

"They will if you keep hanging out at the Blue Dog Bar."

Carter grimaced. "That wasn't my idea. My contact insisted. He thought it would make me nervous to be around so many cops. It did, but not in the way he thought."

"You calling ahead helped," Killian told him. "Jenny put out the word. She's a great girl. Too bad you let that one get away."

"She wasn't for me." Jenny had been great, but he'd

let her go as easily as everyone else. Most of the time he was fine with his life and appreciated the women he'd dated and then walked away from, but sometimes he wondered if there was something wrong with him...a reason he couldn't settle down like everyone else.

"Just as well," his boss said. "With this assignment, you don't need the added pressure of being involved. But when it's over, what next?"

Carter looked at him. "What do you mean? I take the next job."

"Another undercover assignment? Come on, Carter. You passed the tests, you're ready to move up to detective. So what's stopping you? Why do you always turn down the job?"

"I turned down one."

"Most guys would jump at the chance to make detective."

Carter shrugged. "I'll get there."

"Why take the test if you're not interested?"

"I am interested." If the man talking had been anyone but his boss, Carter would have told him to back off.

"Then act like it. Take the next opening. You can't play forever. Maybe it's time to grow up."

Carter glared at Killian. "What I do is damned important. I make a difference."

"You could make a bigger difference as detective. You know it and I know it. So what's holding you back?"

Saturday morning started with complete chaos. Ten five-year-olds running through the open classroom, their parents talking in groups and Rachel sorting through supplies left in the small yard off her classroom.

She knew nothing about lumber or tools, so she wasn't sure if she had everything she was supposed to have. While she could figure out which wood was which from the size, she wasn't sure if she had the right braces or not.

"Need some help?" Carter asked as he stepped out into the yard.

"Desperately," she said and held out her list. "Do I have all this? I've never made a booth before and to be honest, I have no big plans to make one now. That's why you and the parents are here. Well, some of you will help me with the card kits, but that's the easy part. It's mostly sorting and counting."

She was aware she was talking too much, which frequently happened the first time she saw Carter after any kind of absence. She wanted to explain that, technically, it wasn't her fault. There was something about looking at him that unhinged her brain. Something that made her remember what it was like to touch him and kiss him and…

He moved close and smiled at her. "You about wound down?"

If she said no, would he stop her talking in the most interesting way possible?

"Pretty much. The kindergarteners have never had to have a booth before. I was very comfortable in that position. Suddenly, someone decided we were capable, or at least the parents were. I know nothing about building.

Can you take charge of this and coordinate the work? In theory, the build should take no more than two hours."

"I've built cabinets. I can handle a festival booth." He glanced over the instructions. "It'll be fun. Are the kids supposed to help?"

"If they want. I'm going to have some of them with me, putting together our card kits."

"Which are?"

"Greeting cards. Some are preprinted and some can be made by hand with decorations and trims."

He took a step back. "Don't make me do that."

She grinned. "I promise. You can stay out here and be macho with the wood and paint."

"Perfect."

He smiled at her and she felt her insides shimmy a little. Despite her urge to throw herself at him, she drew in a deep breath and walked toward the classroom. "Let's go gather the troops and divide into teams."

Back in the classroom, Rachel explained their two projects and let the parents and kids divide up themselves. She felt someone tugging on the hem of her T-shirt and turned.

"Morning, Christian," she said to the small boy. "Are you excited to help build the booth?"

Christian nodded. "Is he your boyfriend?" he asked, pointing at Carter.

Rachel's mind went blank. Under the circumstances it was a reasonable question and one she should have expected. "Ah, well, to be honest…"

"Yes," Carter said easily.

Christian giggled. "Are you gonna kiss her?"

"Maybe later. If she's very good."

A couple of the mothers exchanged glanced as if they wouldn't mind being rewarded by Carter for excellent behavior.

"Okay, then," Rachel said, ignoring the heat on her cheeks. "Let's get started."

Carter led the construction crew outside while she put the card kit folks to work in the classroom. She had set up several stations for the kids, showing how many of each items went in to the various bags. White cardboard signs showed five buttons inside a bag at one station and three bows in another bag at a different station.

Soon kids and parents alike were counting greeting cards and filling bags. When she was sure everything was going smoothly, she walked to her desk and pulled out her parent list. There were a few she wanted to talk to today. It was more casual than an official parent-teacher conference.

"Helen, do you have a second?" Rachel asked a pretty, dark-haired woman who was helping with the bow counting.

"Sure, Rachel."

Rachel let the way into the classroom next door. It was empty and quiet.

When they were seated on the two adult-sized chairs Rachel had brought in earlier that morning, she leaned forward.

"I'm a little worried about Anastasia. She's a wonderful girl. So bright and friendly and she loves learning. But she's obviously exhausted. She falls asleep during storytime nearly every day."

Helen stiffened. "I don't know what you mean. We put her to bed at nine. That should be enough sleep."

"She's only five. I think an earlier bedtime might help. Does she try to stay up later? Some kids are natural night owls." Rachel didn't think that was the problem, but she'd found it was usually more productive to start by getting the parent on her side than to make an outright accusation.

Helen shook her head. "Anastasia is always ready to go to bed when it's time. In fact, if we've been out after seven, she falls asleep in the car on the way home."

"Then I would suggest moving her bedtime back fifteen minutes every four or five days until you find a time that gives her enough sleep. It's probably going to be about seven-thirty."

Helen's eyes widened. "But that's not possible. She has her classes."

"Hmm, yes. She's mentioned that she has a lot of activities outside of school. Dance, Spanish, some kind of martial arts."

Helen nodded. "Gymnastics, piano, soccer. We have a schedule. Some are in the afternoon, but a few are in the evening. She couldn't attend them and get to bed earlier."

Rachel tried to figure out the most tactful way to make her point. "I think it's wonderful when caring parents take such an interest in their children. I wish all parents were like you. But sometimes kids get overscheduled. Anastasia needs time to just be a little girl. She needs time to play and dream and imagine as well as learn Spanish."

Helen opened her mouth, then closed it. "We have her doing too much, don't we? I've wondered. It's just both Martin and I have siblings who are gross underachievers. We didn't want that for Anastasia. We want her to have every advantage, but also to understand that she needs to push herself."

"Pushing her now won't teach her that lesson," Rachel said gently. "Anastasia is exceptional because of who she is on the inside, not because of what she does. She's not going to be your little girl for a very long time and that goes so quickly. I would hate for you two to miss these special years because your daughter is never home."

"I'll talk to Martin," Helen said. "Maybe we can back off on the classes."

"Don't give them up all together," Rachel said. "It's good to expose her to a few things. Maybe try a couple this semester and next semester try some different ones. Then you can sit down as a family and figure out what you think is important and she likes to do."

"Okay. Thanks."

"You're more than welcome. Anastasia is wonderful. I'm glad she's in my class."

Helen smiled. "I am, too."

The other woman left. Rachel made some notes on her file, then glanced up when Carter walked into the room.

"Impressive," he said. "I came to tell you the booth is coming together, but I didn't want to interrupt. You handled that really well."

His praise made her feel a little bit floaty inside. "Thanks. I'm with the kids for several hours a day. Because I'm not the parent, I can usually see both the good and bad that's happening. Unfortunately, parents tend to get stuck on one or the other."

"Helen got the message."

Rachel closed her file and stood. "I hope so. I hate seeing these kids dragging because their parents plan for them to be the next Secretary General of the United Nations. But balance is tricky to find."

Carter tucked a strand of hair behind her ear. "My mom did a great job at it. We were all convinced we were her favorite. She made us believe we could do anything."

"My parents were like that, too," Rachel said, remembering the loving support they'd offered her. "I wanted to be an astronaut/ballerina and no one ever said it was a dumb idea. Of course I was only twelve and no one takes career plans seriously at that age. There was this one time that they—"

Unexpected tears filled her eyes. Rachel was so surprised, she stopped in midsentence.

"What's wrong?" Carter asked.

"I don't know." She blinked several times, but the tears wouldn't go away. "I was going to say something about my parents, but I know if I do, I'll burst into tears."

"I can handle it."

She sniffed and smiled at the same time. "I appreciate you saying that. It's just I don't understand. I don't cry very much, especially not about the loss of my

An Important Message from the Editors

Dear Reader,

If you'd enjoy reading romance novels with larger print that's easier on your eyes, let us send you TWO FREE HARLEQUIN SUPERROMANCE® NOVELS in our NEW LARGER PRINT EDITION. These books are complete and unabridged, but the type is set about 20% bigger to make it easier to read. Look inside for an actual-size sample.

By the way, you'll also get a surprise gift with your two free books!

Pam Powers

Peel off Seal and Place Inside...

THE RIGHT WOMAN

she'd thought she was fine. It took Daniel's words and Brooke's question to make her realize she was far from a full recovery.

She'd made a start with her sister's help and she intended to go forward now. Sarah felt as if she'd been living in a darkened room and some-one had suddenly opened a door, letting in the fresh air and sunshine. She could feel its warmth slowly seeping into the coldest part of her. The feeling was liberating. She realized it was only a small step and she had a long way to go, but she was ready to face life again with Serena and her family behind her.

All too soon, they were saying goodbye and Sarah experienced a moment of sadness for all the years she and Serena had missed. But they d each other now and that's what she held   sy o

Printed in the U.S.A.
Publisher acknowledges the copyright holder of the excerpt from this individual work as follows:
THE RIGHT WOMAN Copyright © 2004 by Linda Warren. All rights reserved.
® and ™ are trademarks owned and used by the trademark owner and/or its licensee.

The Harlequin Reader Service™ — Here's How It Works:

Accepting your 2 free Harlequin Superromance® books and gift places you under no obligation to buy anything. You may keep the books and gift and return the shipping statement marked "cancel." If you do not cancel, about a month later we'll send you 6 additional Harlequin Superromance larger print books and bill you just $4.94 each in the U.S., or $5.49 each in Canada, plus 25¢ shipping & handling per book and applicable taxes if any.* That's the complete price and — compared to cover prices of $5.75 each in the U.S. and $6.75 each in Canada — it's quite a bargain! You may cancel at any time, but if you choose to continue, every month we'll send you 6 more books, which you may either purchase at the discount price or return to us and cancel your subscription.

*Terms and prices subject to change without notice. Sales tax applicable in N.Y. Canadian residents will be charged applicable provincial taxes and GST.

If offer card is missing write to: Harlequin Reader Service, 3010 Walden Ave., P.O. Box 1867, Buffalo, NY 14240-1867

BUSINESS REPLY MAIL
FIRST-CLASS MAIL   PERMIT NO. 717-003   BUFFALO, NY

POSTAGE WILL BE PAID BY ADDRESSEE

HARLEQUIN READER SERVICE
3010 WALDEN AVE
PO BOX 1867
BUFFALO NY 14240-9952

NO POSTAGE
NECESSARY
IF MAILED
IN THE
UNITED STATES

family. It's been fourteen years. I'm sad they're gone, but I've recovered, emotionally."

"Hey, it happens."

He drew her close and wrapped his arms around her. She let him because, for reasons she couldn't explain, she needed the comfort.

"This is crazy," she murmured against his shoulder as tears trickled down her cheeks. "I have no reason to cry. This is not like me."

"You're having a baby," he said.

She drew back and stared at him. "I hardly think that's a reason to break down when I talk about my parents. I know the situation is stressful, but speaking as someone who is firmly in denial about the whole thing, I can't believe that's why I'm losing it."

She wiped her face and tried to think happy thoughts. Maybe she should get a kitten. A fluffy white one that would play with a ball of yarn. Only the image of it caused her eyes to fill again.

"I'm not saying it's because you're stressed," he said. "It's hormones. Trust me. I have three sisters who have all been pregnant at least twice. You might not want to think about being pregnant, but your body is seriously busy producing all kinds of chemicals. You're reacting to them."

Was that possible?

"Are you saying I'm going to be an emotional basket case for the next seven months?"

"Possibly."

"I'll never survive."

"Sure you will. Besides, I'll be right here. You can cry on my shoulder anytime."

She laughed, which helped ease the need to sob. He cupped her face in his hands and used his thumbs to wipe her cheeks.

"Better?" he asked.

She nodded, then found her gaze lingering on his mouth.

"Yeah," he murmured. "Me, too. Think anyone would mind?"

"Hurry up," a small voice called out. "He's gonna kiss her."

Rachel turned and saw Christian and his friend lurking in the doorway. "Great. An audience."

Carter laughed. "I don't do requests. Rain check?"

"Absolutely."

Chapter Eight

Crissy set the pitcher of iced tea on the table, then put her hands on her hips. "Let me just say for the record, I'm bitter about the lack of wine, okay?"

Noelle smiled. "I'm only twenty. I couldn't drink the wine anyway."

"You could be with us in spirit," Crissy grumbled. "But you're right. So, Rachel, what's your excuse?"

"I'm pregnant."

"I meant for getting pregnant."

Rachel didn't have an actual answer for that. Fortunately the phone rang…again.

Noelle's smile broadened. "That's probably Dev," she murmured. "I'll take it in the other room."

Crissy stared after her. "We've been here less than

two hours and this is his third call. It's amazing he can get any work done."

"I'm thinking he's not," Rachel said, wondering what it would be like to be that in love. She'd wanted that for herself, had tried twice. So what had gone wrong? Did she just have bad taste in men or did she not know how to have a good relationship?

"I'm sure he misses her," Crissy said as she poured Rachel a glass of iced tea. "I still can't believe they're so much in love, but they are. Talk about lucky."

Crissy sounded both happy for her friend and a little wistful, which Rachel could relate to.

"She's glowing," Rachel said. "Now that they know the baby's all right, they can be happy."

"Are you happy?" Crissy asked. "You haven't said much about your own pregnancy."

For good reason, Rachel thought. "I'm doing okay. Physically I don't feel any different. At least not yet. I had an emotional meltdown the other day, which isn't like me, but I guess now I have hormones to deal with." She leaned toward Crissy. "Honestly? I can't seem to get my mind around the fact that I'm having a baby. I've tried to think about it as far as what all I have to plan for and deal with, and when I do I start to panic. It seems easier to ignore the whole thing. But that can't be good, either."

"You have time," Crissy told her. "What? Seven more months? Trust me, as you begin to completely lose control of your body, you'll get that it's real."

Rachel grinned. "Lose control? You make me feel like aliens have invaded and will soon be bursting out."

"Pretty much."

"You have personal experience in the matter?" Rachel asked teasingly.

Crissy shrugged. "I've been doing some reading so I can relate to what Noelle's going through. And now you." She reached in her purse and held up a bottle of water. "But to be on the safe side, I'm avoiding any liquids that come from a tap. What is it with you two?"

"We're just lucky," Noelle said as she walked back into the kitchen and took her seat at the table. "Dev says hi and promises he won't call again until after you guys are gone."

"I'm not a big believer in happy endings," Crissy said, "but looking at you is kinda making me a believer. You look good in love."

"Thanks. I feel good. Now I just have to get you two married off."

Crissy scooted back her chair. "I'm fine being single. Did I mention my charming cat? He's more than enough company, thank you very much. I hate first dates enough to never want to go on one again!"

"You're going to be a tough one," Noelle said. "I thought we'd start with someone easier." She turned to Rachel. "So how's Carter?"

Rachel laughed. "He's fine, but you're wasting your time setting us up. It's not going to happen."

"Why not?" Noelle passed around the large bowl of Chinese chicken salad. "You said he's a great guy."

"He is. He's funny and charming and I think he's dated nearly every age-appropriate woman in a tristate area."

Noelle nodded. "You don't think he's good husband material."

Rachel considered the statement. "Actually, I think he is. He cares a lot about his family. They're all wonderful. He's responsible and caring. He helped me out with my fall festival booth last weekend, which was great."

"He sounds perfect," Crissy said as she took a roll. "Which makes me instantly not want to trust him. But I'm the cynical member of the team. What's your excuse?"

"For one thing, he's made it really clear that he's not interested in anything long-term. Carter doesn't believe in romantic love. Not for himself anyway."

Noelle dismissed the problem with a flick of her fingers. "That just means he hasn't met the right someone yet. Which could be you. But I don't understand. Doesn't it bother you that he doesn't want to get married for the sake of the baby?"

"Not really," Rachel admitted. "I know that decision was right for you, but it's not right for me. I don't need to be married to have a child. Carter will be part of the baby's life and that's enough."

Crissy and Noelle exchanged a glance that told Rachel they'd been discussing this without her.

"You've always talked about wanting a family," Crissy said slowly. "I thought you meant in the traditional sense. Husband and kids."

"I do want that. Just not with Carter."

Noelle took some salad for herself. "At the risk of sounding stupid, why not? If he's all that you said, how can you keep from falling in love with him?"

"I just can."

Rachel had been in love twice, or so she'd thought. She'd agreed to marry two terrific guys, only to have second thoughts a few weeks later. She'd hated hurting them by ending the relationships, but she hadn't been willing to go forward with their plans when her feelings had changed.

This was when she missed her mother the most. She wanted to ask questions about her parents' courtship and hear how they'd known that each other was the one. She wanted to be told that there was nothing wrong with her, that when she met the right guy, she would just know.

Apparently Carter wasn't that guy. He was wonderful and she liked being with him and she still went weak remembering their one night together, but was that enough to hold a marriage together? Shouldn't there be some defining moment when she just *knew?*

"I'll find Mr. Right," Rachel said. "He's out there."

"Waiting," Crissy said with a grin. "Longing for you. Desperate and needy."

Rachel rolled her eyes. "Stop it or I'll spike your bottled water with something from the tap and then you'll get pregnant, too."

"Never," Crissy said firmly.

The morning of the fall festival promised perfect Southern California weather. Blue skies and a cool start to the day with afternoon temperatures in the low eighties.

Rachel had arrived before eight to supervise the setup. The booth had turned out great, with bright colors and plenty of room for the sale of greeting cards. Now she checked the inventory against the numbers on her master list and made a note that she had to count the change.

"Coffee," Brady's mom said as she walked over with a tray filled with steaming paper cups. "I stopped on the way."

"Thanks," Rachel said as she took one of the small cups and set it on the booth. She'd never been much of a coffee drinker and these days she was avoiding caffeine, but it seemed easier to take the drink and get rid of it discreetly at a later time than to explain why she was refusing.

"I'm excited," Brady's mom continued. "He's our oldest, so this is the first time we're able to get involved in school activities. I can't wait to get started."

Rachel knew there were two other younger children at home. "Okay, but hold on to that enthusiasm," she teased. "We don't want you burning out before the baby hits kindergarten."

"I won't," she promised.

"Morning, ladies."

Rachel didn't have to turn around and see the speaker to recognize the voice. "Carter," she said. "You're early."

"It's the fall festival. How could I resist?"

How could *she?* He looked good in his worn jeans and dark T-shirt. Why was it a man could step out of the shower, pull on any old thing and look fabulous while women had to sweat makeup and stylish clothes to achieve any kind of gorgeous?

"You have a burning need for greeting cards?" she asked.

"I might. You never know."

"Carter? Is that you?"

Rachel stepped back to avoid being pushed aside as a woman flung herself at Carter, wrapping her arms around him as she pressed her body against his.

"It is you. Ohmygosh! I can't believe it. What are you doing here?"

Rachel blinked. "Eden?"

The woman glanced at Rachel and grinned. "Oh, hi, Rachel."

Eden Baker was one of the teachers at Rachel's school and obviously another of Carter's exes.

Carter reached up and carefully loosened Eden's grip from around his neck. "Good to see you, Eden. How's John?"

"He's great." Eden released Carter and stepped back. She smiled at Rachel. "Sorry. I didn't mean to be rude. I was just so shocked to see Carter here. I could never get him to come to any school events. It's been what? Five years?"

"About that," he said.

Eden's smile widened. "I'm a happily married woman now and I wouldn't change a thing, but we had some good times." She patted Rachel's arm. "Enjoy him, honey. Enjoy him for all of us."

Rachel watched Eden head back to her booth, then she turned to Carter. "I'm thinking maybe you could just give me a list. You know, names, occupations, addresses, so I can be prepared for the next round of women I'm going to meet."

Carter shuffled his feet and shoved his hands into his front pockets. "There aren't that many."

"Really? I seem unable to leave the house with you without us running into someone you used to date. And I use the term 'date' very loosely."

All his exes weren't excited to see him because he'd known how to pick a great movie.

"Are you mad?" he asked.

"No, not mad. Just out of my element. I've never known a guy like you."

"Is that a bad thing?" he asked.

He was so obviously uncomfortable, she wanted to laugh. He could have strutted around and bragged about his conquests. The fact that he didn't made her willing to deal with all the Edens and Jennys she was bound to meet.

"I'm thinking you should give lessons to less fortunate males," she teased. "It would be a great side job. Think of the money you'd make."

"You're exaggerating," he told her. "I—"

"Carter? Carter Brockett? As I live and breathe, is that you, honey?"

Rachel patted him on the arm. "I'll go take care of my booth. You handle the fans."

By that afternoon, the festival was officially a success. Rachel went over her inventory and was pleased to see they'd already sold about eighty percent of the greeting-card kits. Parents were showing up on time to man the booth, the kids were having a blast—running through the playground and getting in the way—and money was being made for the school.

Carter had ducked out before lunch, although he'd promised to return later. Now Rachel found herself watching for him, which she didn't like. Their deal of pretend dating didn't have any room for the real thing.

Still, she scanned the crowd, then smiled when she saw a familiar older woman heading in her direction.

Rachel walked into the main path to greet Nina Brockett.

"What are you doing here?" she asked as Carter's mom gave her a hug.

"I always come to the fall festival. I have grandchildren, you know."

"I do know. I've met nearly all of them. Your entire family has stopped by to say hi."

Rachel hadn't expected their appearance but had enjoyed it. The Brocketts were obviously willing to take her in and accept her as one of them. Unfortunately, their warmth left her feeling guilty about her secret plan with Carter.

"So what are you selling?" Nina asked as she moved to the booth. "Oh, cards. Very nice."

"Um, you might want to buy something else," Rachel told her. "All three of your daughters bought cards, so you're all at risk of sending each other exactly the same one."

"Still, I want to support your class." She leaned close. "Children are a blessing and I love every one of mine, but grandchildren are the reward. You wait. You'll see what I mean. Have you seen Carter?"

"He was here this morning to help me set up."

"Good. He talked about how important the festival was to you. How it's the major fund-raiser for the school. He asked us all to come and stop by."

Had he? That was unexpected, but nice to hear.

"Carter's a good man," his mother said. "He's always thinking about the people he cares about. He's responsible, too."

Rachel silently groaned at the obvious matchmaking. "Nina, you don't have to sell him to me."

Nina smiled. "Of course I do. I want to make sure you both fall in love and get married. Not just for the baby, although he or she is going to need a name, but for yourself. There's nothing better than a happy marriage. I know. I had ten wonderful years with Carter's father."

Rachel held in the need to point out that her baby would have a name even if it wasn't Carter's and decided it was much safer to shift the topic of conversation.

"You've been a widow for a long time. Didn't you ever want to remarry?"

"I thought about it," Nina told her. "I wanted a man around for my children. I decided that when I fell in love again, I'd marry, but not for any other reason. Like you."

Rachel blinked. "Excuse me?"

"Carter mentioned you'd been engaged before but had broken things off. I'm glad. That means you're sensible *and* romantic. A good combination."

While she appreciated the praise, she wasn't sure she deserved it. "I made a mistake with each of them," Rachel admitted. "I thought I was in love, which is why I said yes. But I wasn't."

"Exactly. Romantic enough to see the possibilities and sensible enough to know what was required to make things work. Now you have Carter. He's my son so I'm biased, but where are you going to do better?"

Nina patted her hand and walked toward the booth. Rachel stayed where she was as the other woman's question echoed in her brain.

Where *was* she going to do better? Carter was everything she'd ever wanted in a man and she practically became a puddle every time they were close. So why wasn't she pushing for a real relationship? Why was she content to keep her distance?

She didn't have any answers, and it was a little unsettling. When she tried to dig deeper, emotionally, she found only that dark scary place that made her want to ignore the whole issue.

Love meant loss. She'd learned the lesson early and well when her family had been killed and she'd been left totally alone. Since then she'd found the courage to let some people in to her life. Her friends, her kids. She could care about them and survive the fear. But anything more was out of the question. The potential for loss was too great—she wouldn't risk it. Which was why Carter was perfect for her. He didn't want any more than she could give.

* * *

"I confess, I never thought of the 'after' part," Rachel said as Carter took the end of a hammer to the booth and started pulling out nails.

"What did you think happened?" he asked. "That the festival would end and the booths would disappear?"

"Sure. I thought they went back to their festival booth village and lived happily with others of their own kind."

He looked at her. "Sometimes you're a little weird, you know that?"

"I've been told."

She ached from the long day spent at the booth. She'd had a full contingent of parents to handle the sales, but she'd been in charge. Except for a quick lunch break, she'd been on her feet since seven that morning.

"I need a long bath," she said as she moved her feet to shoulder-width apart, then bent over. Her fingers curled against the asphalt of the playground. She put her palms on the rough surface and pressed down until she felt a stretch in the back of her legs.

After grabbing her left ankle, she pulled herself to the side, then repeated the movement on her right side. When she straightened, she found Carter staring at her.

"What?" she asked.

"You're really limber."

She grinned. "Yes, I am. I haven't had much time for dance class lately, but I do my stretching."

He muttered something and went back to work on disassembling the booth.

Had that been a flicker of hunger in his eyes, she

wondered happily. Did he, too, feel the pull between them? She started to tease him about it, then stopped herself.

She and Carter had a good working plan. Getting intimate again would only complicate the situation and neither of them wanted that. She was still feeling a little unsettled by his mother's visits and her claims that Carter was the perfect man. Or if not perfect, then at least perfect for her.

"Your family all stopped by," she said to change the subject. "Your mom told me you'd mentioned the festival to them and they came by to be supportive."

He twisted the booth into three separate parts. "It's a fund-raiser. I wanted to help."

"The booth building and destruction was more than enough. You didn't have to do that, but thank you for saying something. It was nice."

"They like you." He tossed the smaller pieces into the back of his truck.

"I like them. You're lucky, Carter."

"I know."

He straightened and suddenly they were standing way too close together. His dark eyes seem to draw her in, so that she took a step toward him without even meaning to.

His broad shoulders offered the perfect resting place for her hands, so it wasn't really her fault that she put them there. He was warm and strong and she couldn't seem to stop looking at his mouth.

Nearly everyone had already left and there was only

the call of a few birds in the playground. To Rachel, it felt as if they were alone in the world.

He rested his hands on her waist. "We have to stop doing this," he told her.

"Why?" she asked.

"Hell if I can remember."

And then he kissed her. He bent down and claimed her mouth with a possessive heat that branded her. Even as she wrapped her arms around his neck, she surged toward him, her body moving without permission. As if it had no choice but to be next to him. His thighs pressed against hers, his chest flattened her breasts and she knew she could stay in his embrace forever.

She parted and he swept inside her mouth. His tongue touched hers with a slow, erotic stroke. The thrill stole her breath. She clung to him, letting him claim her, then following him back and claiming him.

Need grew until she had to have him or die. She was already aroused and hungry. There were—

The sound of a child's laughter echoed in the late afternoon. She told herself it didn't matter, that she was allowed to kiss Carter, but she didn't quite believe it and even if she did, he'd already pulled back.

"Great idea, bad timing," he said.

His eyes were dark with passion. Wanting tightened his expression until she knew for certain he was a man in need.

She wanted to know that his desire was specifically for her. That she was different from all those who had come before. Except she wasn't, and she couldn't be. None of this was real, remember?

"You all right?" he asked.

She nodded. "I get a little confused. It's the kissing. You do it better than anyone I've ever, well, kissed."

"You're pretty good, yourself."

"So speaks the voice of experience."

He winced. "Ouch."

She smiled. "Come on, Carter, you can't avoid the truth. You've dated more women than the average professional football team."

"I doubt that."

"Close enough. I've had two serious boyfriends in my life and I was engaged to each of them."

"Not at the same time, right?"

Even hungry for his kiss and not sure how to reconcile what was happening, she liked that he could still make her laugh.

"Not at the same time. There were a couple of years between them. My point is I've never done the casual thing before."

"Probably for the best, considering what happened that first night."

She touched her stomach. "Right. So we should stay with our plan. Pretend dating." And that meant there should be a whole lot less kissing.

"I can do that," he said.

"Me, too. So we don't have a problem."

"Not even a little one."

"Good."

"Great."

They stared at each other and she fought against the need to throw herself at him. Just one more night, she thought. One long, slow, sexy night in his bed, his arms. She wanted his hands on her body, his tongue in her mouth and his...

"Rachel?" His voice sounded strangled.

"Yes?" Was that breathy whisper really her?

"You gotta stop thinking like that. I can't stand it. In fact, why don't you head home? I'll finish up here."

She almost said no. She almost issued the invitation she sensed he would accept. But then what? Could she make love with Carter a second time and not get emotionally involved?

What if the worst happened? What if she fell for him? He was the guy most likely to walk away, which would leave her emotionally broken and bleeding on the side of the road.

"I can't do this," she told him.

"I'm not asking you to."

"Right. You're not."

She made the rational choice then and collected her car keys. Then she walked across the parking lot and into the relative safety of her small car.

Once she'd started the engine, she drove directly home without once looking back. She knew if she looked back, she would turn around. And if she turned around, she might be lost forever.

Chapter Nine

Rachel handed over her car keys and walked into the waiting room of the local auto repair shop. She was diligent about regular oil changes for her little car, although this might be one of the last ones she'd have to have done. The two-seater convertible wasn't practical for a single mom with a newborn. She would have to start looking around for something bigger. Maybe a four-door of some kind. Something with a good safety record and side airbags.

Maybe Carter could help her find one that was…

She flopped down onto one of the plastic chairs and held in a groan. Not Carter. She hadn't seen or talked to him since the fall festival the previous weekend and she preferred things that way. Better to take some time and get him off her mind and out of her system.

She'd been doing a pretty good job, too, not thinking about him more than three or four hundred times a day. Now if she could get that down to an even hundred, she could consider herself on the road to recovery.

The problem was she missed him. He was so good to have around. Not just because he was gorgeous—which he was—but because he was fun and charming and caring and thoughtful. And those qualities made her once again wonder why she was so dead set on avoiding anything personal with him.

But every time she thought about talking to him about something more than their pretend relationship, she felt shaky and afraid. Nope, this was better.

She opened a home decorating magazine, but couldn't concentrate on any of the articles. Then she flipped through a travel magazine, but that didn't hold her interest, either. She was the only customer and knew she wouldn't be waiting long, but still she felt restless. Giving in the need to move, she walked out of the waiting room and paced the sidewalk of the main road.

This was the part of town that catered to those with cars. There were several body shops, a place that sold custom wheels and a motorcycle sales-and-repair place. She stared at the latter because it made her think of Carter. That's where he was working. Or at least pretend work while undercover.

Pretend work, pretend relationship. Was anything in his life real?

A beautiful blonde stepped out of the sales office and onto the sidewalk. Three men followed her. They were all talking intently. Then a fourth man joined them and Rachel nearly shrieked in surprise. It was Carter!

She glanced around, not sure what she should do. Not call out to him, of course. That was his police world and she wasn't supposed to know him.

She turned and hurried to the waiting room. When she was safely back in the small, glass space, she hid behind a magazine, while watching the ongoing conversation. The men seemed to come to some kind of agreement, because they all shook hands. Then Carter put his arm around the blonde and gave her a long, lingering kiss on the lips.

The magazine fell to the floor. Rachel half rose, then sank back onto the seat. She blinked several times, but the image didn't go away. There was Carter sharing a very intimate moment with another woman.

Her chest ached, it was difficult to breathe and she had the strongest urge to cry. Only this time the tears wouldn't be brought on by pregnancy hormones. Instead they would be the result of anger and betrayal.

How could he do that? How could he kiss someone else? They were…

What? she thought. What were they doing? Not dating. Not for real. It was all fake, done for the benefit of his family. Hadn't she made it clear that she didn't want anything from him? Hadn't she made it clear she wasn't any more interested in getting involved than he was? So none of this should matter.

Except it did and she hurt.

"Hey, Rach, the car's done. Oil's changed and everything else checks out fine."

She turned toward her mechanic. "Thanks, Evan. What do I owe you?"

Twenty minutes later she found herself driving around town. Her work day was finished, she was tired and confused and the best place for her was home. Only she couldn't seem to make herself go in that direction, so she made turns until she pulled in to the parking lot of the Blue Dog Bar.

She stared at the neon sign, then at the door. The need to go inside got stronger and stronger until she finally climbed out of her car and walked across the parking lot.

It took her eyes a second to adjust from the bright afternoon to the dimness of the bar. She glanced around and saw Jenny drying glasses. Rachel wasn't sure why she thought Carter's ex-girlfriend could help. Maybe it was because Jenny knew the man but seemed to have let him go and moved on. Maybe it was because Carter's sisters and mother liked and trusted her. Maybe it was the first symptom of a pregnancy-induced insanity. Regardless, Rachel made her way to the bar and slid onto a stool.

Jenny put down her dishtowel. "Hi, Rachel. This is a surprise. Looking for Carter again?"

"No. I have his cell number now."

Jenny grinned. "Good for you. So what's up? You want something to drink?" Her gaze dipped to Rachel's midsection. "A seltzer or soda?"

"Just water, please." She glanced around at the quiet room and remembered how busy it had been that first night, when she'd come here with Diane. "How long have you worked here?"

"Mostly all my life," Jenny said. "My dad owns the place. Or he used to. I'm buying him out, a little every month. Dan jokes that when we finally own the place outright, we'll license the name and become a chain. I'm thinking one bar is plenty." She handed Rachel a tall glass of water with ice and a slice of lemon. "Here you go."

"Thanks." Rachel sipped the water. "I, ah, I'm not sure why I'm here. I didn't know where else to go. You know Carter and you seem nice."

Jenny shook her head. "That doesn't sound good. Is there a problem?"

"I don't know. Maybe. I was getting my oil changed and I went for a walk while I was waiting. I saw Carter across the street with a bunch of guys. There was a blonde there, too. Tall and really beautiful. He kissed her. Seriously kissed her. For a long time. I know what he does and I know this is probably some part of that, but still…"

Jenny pulled up a stool and sat down. "Carter doesn't cheat. He has a lot of flaws, but that's not one of them. He doesn't lie or even bend the truth. If you two are together and he was kissing someone else, then it was about work. Trust me. I've known him for a lot of years. Despite plenty of opportunity, he's never once strayed."

If he were in a relationship, Rachel thought glumly. But they weren't. Not really. So who was the woman?

Jenny leaned toward her. "Look, I'm sorry about before. That I told his mom you were pregnant. I didn't know you and I wanted to protect Carter. He's important to me. Now, I kinda wish I'd kept my mouth shut."

Rachel smiled. "It worked out okay, but thanks for apologizing. I adore his family, but they're a lot to deal with."

"I know. That's what's so great about him. Listen, Carter is terrific, but there will always be women in his life. His family, his old girlfriends, even me. He adores women and they adore him."

"I've met a few of the old girlfriends. Some of them are scary."

"I know." Jenny smiled. "There were a couple who made it clear that they wanted him back and they didn't care that we were together."

"I ran across one of those, too. They're everywhere. He says he's sworn off women before, but with so many exes strolling around, I don't see how that's possible."

"They were short breaks," Jenny told her. "Sometimes measured in hours."

Rachel ran her finger down the length of the glass. "What happened with you two? Why did you break up?"

"Honestly? I wanted him to fall madly in love with me and he never did. I don't think Carter's ever been in love. Not romantically. He thinks he's immune, but I believe he's going to fall hard one day and I can't wait to see it. Maybe you'll be the one."

Rachel had her doubts about that. "He's had plenty of opportunity."

"If you're going to be with him, you have to be able to handle what happened before. Those other women exist."

"So I've seen. Some of them can't seem to let go. You did, though."

"I was pretty broken up when Carter and I split, but it worked out for the best. Dan is amazing. If I'd stayed with Carter, I never would have met him."

"But you're still a part of Carter's life. Isn't that strange?"

"It was at first," Jenny admitted with a smile. "But after a while I realized I missed his family more than I missed him. Liz and I had become close. So I just butted in. No one minded, least of all Carter. Which is good. I'm the only child of a single dad. I never had brothers or sisters. Now I have both. The Brockett clan is good at taking in strays, and I'm happy to be one of them."

Strays? Rachel had never thought of herself that way but she supposed she fit the description, which didn't make her comfortable.

"You should talk to Carter," Jenny said. "Ask him about the kiss."

"But that would be so logical and mature. I don't think I'm ready for that."

"It's your call. Better to get the question answered than wonder."

"It's not a big deal," Rachel assured her. "We're not...we're not that serious."

"Really? For someone who isn't serious, you seem plenty upset."

"I'm fine."

"Are you trying to convince me or yourself?"

* * *

Carter thought about calling first, but he didn't want to get into it on the phone with Rachel. So he swung by his mother's house, picked up lasagna, garlic bread and salad, then showed up at Rachel's place a little after five.

"I hope you haven't eaten yet," he said when she opened the door.

She wore her hair back in a ponytail and her face was scrubbed clean of makeup. He liked seeing the pale freckles on her nose and the tiny scar by her right eyebrow. She wore a T-shirt and old jeans, an intriguing contrast to her usually prissy teacher clothes. Not that he hadn't learned to appreciate the subtle sexiness of prissy.

"What?" she asked as she stepped back to let him in. "I haven't eaten. I was going to have a salad or something. Why are you here with dinner? We didn't have plans."

He carried dinner into her kitchen and set it on the counter. "I've had five phone calls in the past hour," he told her. "Word travels fast."

She groaned. "Jenny called one of your sisters?"

"Two of them, actually. They called the third and my mom." He took her hands in his and rubbed her fingers. "I was working. Ellie is my partner. That's all. We're posing as a couple for this assignment. I would never cheat on you."

She made a halfhearted attempt to pull her hands free. When he didn't let her, she sighed.

"It's fine. I understand. Plus, it's not like we're really dating."

For once he couldn't tell what she was thinking. "Whatever we are, that can't have been fun to see."

She shrugged. "I was shocked and then I wasn't sure I had the right to be upset. Not that I was."

He tugged her a little closer and stared into her eyes. "I'm sorry you were upset. I really am doing this for work."

Her mouth twisted slightly. "Oh, sure. Talk about a yucky assignment. She's beautiful."

"She's okay. But I don't think of her that way. She's my partner. It's about as exciting as kissing one of my sisters. Besides, even if I wanted to like it, I couldn't. Her husband is a big guy and he'd beat the crap out of me."

That earned him a smile.

"I'm okay," she told him. "Thanks for worrying, but you don't have to."

"Are you sure? Because I grew up with three sisters. I know how to dig up a good worry on command."

The smile widened. "Maybe next time." She tilted her head. "Are you mad because I talked to Jenny?"

"You're allowed to talk to anyone you want."

"In theory. I wasn't spying on you or trying to dig up secrets. Honestly, I just didn't know what to think."

"Did she help you feel better?"

"Sort of. We talked about your past."

Not good, he thought glumly. "You can't hold that against me."

"I'm not. However, I think there should be some kind

of club, or support group. We could come up with a name and hold meetings. You could be a guest speaker."

He released her hands. "You *are* upset."

"I'm really not. It's just you're not like any other guy I've ever known."

That didn't sound pleasant. "It's the volume thing," he muttered, knowing he wasn't going to apologize for dating a lot. Despite the gnawing in his gut, he hadn't done anything wrong. "Look, when I'm with a woman, she's the one I'm interested in. Not anyone else."

"I know that. You're loyal and honest and from what I can tell, you don't have any flaws."

"That's what I've been saying for years," he told her. "No one listens."

She smiled again. "Okay, you do have flaws, but they're not typical ones."

"Which would be?"

"I don't know. An obsession about sports. An inability to show up on time."

"I'm prompt."

"Yes, you are." She shook her head. "I don't even know what we're talking about anymore."

"We're talking about the fact that I'm sorry you were upset before. I should have told you about Ellie."

"It wasn't your fault. It was just…weird."

"Recoverable weird?" he asked.

Her green eyes sparkled with amusement and pleasure. "Yes. Recoverable weird."

He gave an exaggerated exhale. "Good, because the other kind of weird is just not for me."

"You're a little crazy," she said.

"Also a good thing. See—I have so many good qualities. I'm prompt and charming and totally into the person I'm with."

"So if this was real, you'd be totally into me?"

Awareness filled the room. Carter had a three-second battle with himself and need won over noble sacrifice. "I'm already totally into you."

Her eyes widened but she didn't look away. "You don't have to be. We're just trying to fake out your family."

He moved closer. "Is that all? So nothing else is required?"

"Not a thing." This time she eased toward him.

"So anything not related to faking out my family would be a waste of time and energy?" he asked as he put one hand on her shoulder and touched her cheek with the other.

"Totally."

"Something I can relate to."

He kissed her. Rachel had known he was going to. In fact, she'd counted on it. Maybe it *was* a complete waste of time and energy, but she couldn't think of a better way to do it.

Her body clenched in anticipation of the pleasure she always experienced when he put his mouth on hers. She wrapped her arms around him and leaned against his hard, muscled body. Her breath caught, her lips parted and she prepared herself for the ride.

He claimed her with a kiss that touched her down to her itty-bitty red blood cells. Heat poured through her making her tremble and want to rip off clothes. Desire exploded until she wondered if a kiss was going to be enough. If this time she would need more.

He plunged his tongue into her mouth. She met him stroke for stroke, savoring the tingles that accompanied every brush, every inch of contact.

Apparently he felt the pressing need, too, because he dropped his hands to her hips and urged her closer. She pulsed against him. The second she did so, she felt the hardness of his arousal. Her body remembered what it had been like to be claimed by him and she trembled.

He kept his hands on her hips, holding her in place, then rubbed against her. She desperately wanted to wrap her legs around him so he could do exactly that to her hot, swollen center.

He kissed his way along her jaw to her neck, and then down her neck. "We have dinner," he whispered against her skin. Quick flicks of his tongue followed by little bites punctuated his sentence. "Lasagna."

"I love lasagna," she moaned.

"So we could stop and eat."

Stop? Was he kidding? She slid her hands under his loose T-shirt and rested her palms on his bare belly. "Do you really want to stop?"

He raised his head and grinned. "I think the pasta will keep."

"Me, too."

That decided, she expected him to pull her into his arms again. Instead, he grabbed her hand and led her down the hallway. When they were in her bedroom, he sat on the bed and pulled off his boots. After he'd let them fall on the floor, he tugged her between his legs and unfastened the button at the waistband of her jeans.

"I've only seen you in dresses and skirts," he said. "Long dresses and skirts."

"They're more practical for my job."

She'd been planning on saying more. She had a whole speech that defended her wardrobe, but just then he pressed an openmouthed kiss to her belly and she forgot everything, even how to breathe.

"I'm not complaining," he said against her skin. "I like it. Very old-fashioned, but sexy. Still, the jeans are nice. I like seeing the curve of your hips and butt. I like thinking about touching those curves."

Her throat went dry, while other parts of her got really, really wet. "You've only been here about twenty minutes. How could you have thought all that so fast?"

He tugged her jeans and panties down to nearly her knees. "I thought it all in the first thirty seconds."

Was that true? On the heels of the question came the realization she was kind of trapped. And naked. She couldn't step out of her jeans and she was still dressed on the top half. This was not how she'd imagined things going between them.

"Carter, I…"

"Trust me."

He bent toward her and used his fingers to gently part her. She nearly lost her balance and had to put her hands on his shoulders to steady herself. Then, while she tried to figure out how to explain that she wasn't very comfortable, he licked her.

The combination of being slightly off balance, seminaked and the erotic kiss nearly did her in. She gasped as she felt him lick her again. Just a quick, wet caress that made everything else seem unimportant.

"Okay, yeah," he murmured. "More of that."

He moved his hands to her waist, then eased her around until she was on her back on the bed. Her jeans and panties went flying, then he was between her legs and she knew that she would soon be lost.

He kissed her there as perfectly as he kissed her everywhere else. Openmouthed, slow-moving and thorough. He explored her, teasing, circling, touching until he found all the places that made her gasp and squirm and beg. Just when she started to think this was a game for him, he settled over her center and picked a rhythm that made the bottoms of her feet burn.

Over and over, he touched her. As her body tensed, he moved a little faster, making her push them to the next level. She began to pulse her hips as every part of her focused on the perfect pleasure.

Her breathing quickened. She tossed her head from side to side. Nothing had ever felt so good.

Then, just as she knew the end was as inevitable as the tide, he slipped two fingers inside of her. The unexpected fullness pushed her over the edge and she lost herself in her climax.

Her release poured through her. It went on and on, making her writhe and cry out and beg him to never stop. Finally the shudders slowed enough for her to catch her breath and open her eyes.

He'd braced himself on one arm and was lightly kissing her stomach. When he looked up, she saw the fire in his eyes and knew he was a man on the edge.

"Don't feel you have to wait," she told him.

He hesitated about an eighth of a second, then unfastened his belt and his jeans and pushed them, and his boxers, down.

"One day we're going to do it like regular people," he said as he positioned himself between her still trembling thighs. "You know, get naked first. Have a conversation."

She reached down and guided him inside of her.

He was thick and hard and he filled her until she knew she was going to have to come again.

"Conversation," she gasped as he plunged in again, "is highly overrated."

Chapter Ten

Rachel woke up to find bright sunlight flooding her bedroom and a heavy arm draped across her stomach. She felt a delicious combination of contentment and exhaustion. Despite the fact that she'd slept in, she'd barely gotten four hours of sleep in the night. She would be dragging all day. But as the reason for the dragging was fairly spectacular, she wasn't about to complain.

She rolled on her side and saw Carter already awake and watching her.

"Morning," he murmured.

"Morning."

She ran her fingers across the stubble on his jaw, then fingered the stud earring.

"Such a bad boy," she told him.

"Smile when you say that."

She laughed. "I'm pretty sure I'm smiling about everything. What you do with a woman could be considered illegal in several states. I don't think one man is allowed to have that much sexual power."

"I can handle it."

He could sure handle her.

He kissed the palm of her hand, then rolled onto his back. "What's the plan for today? Do you have a lot to do? I'm open. Maybe we could do something together."

Her insides gave a little shimmy. "That would be nice," she said carefully, not wanting to appear too enthused. Hanging out was just that. Two friends spending time together. It didn't mean anything, except maybe the possibility of a repeat encounter in bed.

"Shopping," he said, glancing at her. "Women like shopping."

She laughed. "Or we could go to a movie."

"That sounds good. I like movie popcorn." He pulled on her hand, drawing her closer. "Or we could stay in bed. I'm kinda tired. What about you?"

Before she could answer, there was a knock on her front door. Rachel glanced at the clock. It was only a little after nine. She didn't usually get visitors. All her friends phoned rather than dropped by.

She sat up and grabbed her robe, then slipped into it and tied the belt.

"I have no idea who that is," she said as she walked into the living room.

"I do," Carter muttered from the bedroom.

He couldn't possibly know who—

Rachel opened her front door to find Nina Brockett on her plant-filled front balcony.

"I know, I know," Nina said with a bright smile as she passed over a covered basket and stepped inside. "I'm interrupting. Carter's always saying I should call instead of coming by. But it's so much nicer to talk in person. Besides, when I went to Carter's house and he wasn't home, I knew just where he was going to be and I was right."

Rachel opened her mouth, then closed it. Heat flooded her cheeks and she knew she was blushing.

"I, ah…" She pressed her lips together and struggled for control. "Good morning."

"Morning, dear." Nina tapped the basket. "Cinnamon rolls. Carter's favorite. Don't let them get cold."

Carter walked out of the bedroom. He'd pulled on jeans and his shirt. "Mama, you gotta stop doing this."

"Doing what? A mother isn't allowed to talk to her only son? I knocked. Where's the crime?"

He leaned against the door frame and sighed heavily. "Okay, fine. What are you doing here?"

"My water heater is broken. Just like that, it stopped working. Gordon is already off buying me a new one, but he's going to need your help putting it in."

"You could have called," he told her.

"You weren't home and I didn't know if you would be going home to get the message. Besides, I don't have Rachel's number."

"Cell phone, Mama," Carter said. "You could have called my cell phone."

"Oh. I didn't think of that." Nina smiled again. "Besides, it was a lovely drive over here and I'm happy to see you two getting along. It makes an old woman very happy."

"You're not an old woman," Carter said. "You're going to outlive us all."

"Don't say that. No mother wants to outlive her children. Now you two enjoy the cinnamon rolls. Carter, you should call Gordon and see when he'll need you."

With that, she waved and left.

Rachel carefully closed the front door and then crossed to the sofa. As she sank onto the cushions, she covered her face with her hands.

"I'm so embarrassed," she whispered. "That was your mother. She knows what we were doing."

"Oh, yeah. She's real clear on that." He took the basket from her and set it on the coffee table. "Rachel, it's okay."

"It's not. She's your *mother.*"

He sat next to her. His mouth twitched slightly and she guessed he was trying not to smile.

"You think this is funny?" she asked in outrage.

"It's not that big a deal. She knows about the baby, so she's probably not shocked about the sex thing."

Oh, yeah. Good point, but still. "It's just wrong. I felt so awful."

"Don't. She's the one who barged in here. This is your home." He grimaced. "Now it's going to have to be one hell of a fight to convince her we've broken up."

Broken up? Then she remembered. This wasn't real. She and Carter weren't a couple. They were just two people having a baby and trying to convince his family that they were involved, so they could end things later and get back to their original plan of just being two people having a baby.

"We'll need witnesses," she said.

"And a script."

He was being funny, but suddenly she didn't feel like laughing. Nothing about this situation was turning out how she'd thought. Carter's family wasn't supposed to matter, but she found herself hating the thought of Nina thinking less of her. Carter wasn't supposed to be important, yet she wasn't sure she was ready for the breakup they'd planned. Which meant what? That she wanted this to be real? That she wanted to get involved?

No way. Not with him. How could she be with a man who had dated nearly every single woman on the planet? He'd made it clear he didn't want a relationship with her, so she'd better get the idea out of her head.

But wouldn't getting involved with the father of her child be the most logical choice?

The following Thursday, Rachel left work a half hour early and headed for her car. She felt as if an entire team of butterflies had taken up residence in her stomach and were currently arguing on the best way to fly in formation. She was shaky and scared and telling herself that everything was fine, but it didn't seem to be helping.

Ever since she'd made the appointment with her

doctor, she'd had a barely controllable urge to burst into tears. Not because she was especially nervous about the baby—having a child was still something she thought in her head rather than felt in her heart. Instead, she wrestled with the terror of being alone.

Although she'd lost her parents fourteen years ago, she still missed them. At the oddest times she longed for one or the other to be with her. Today it was her mother. She wanted familiar arms to hold her close and say everything was going to be all right. She wanted to hear stories of her mother's pregnancies and births. She wanted a connection to family.

Maybe she should have called Noelle or Crissy, she thought as she drove toward the medical building. Both of them would have been happy to be with her. Noelle was experiencing pregnancy firsthand. But she, Rachel, hadn't wanted to be a bother.

"Talk about dumb," she murmured as she parked and got out of her car. "This was not the time to be noble."

Next time, she promised herself. Next time she would call her friends. Besides, this was only a first appointment. She would be fine.

She walked into the four-story building and started for the elevator, only to come to a complete stop. There, in the center of the lobby, stood Nina, Merry and Liz.

Rachel stared at Carter's mother and sisters. "What are you doing here?" she asked, a little surprised at the coincidence.

Nina shrugged her shoulders. "When I was over on Saturday, I happened to notice the note you'd written about your doctor's appointment. I know, I know, I'm meddling. So sue me. I tried to forget you were coming here, but I couldn't. I know you don't have any family and this is your first baby. I couldn't stand for you to be here alone."

"We wanted to come, too," Merry said, giving Rachel a hug. "Shelly's sorry she couldn't make it, but the sitter we hired got the flu and she offered to stay with all the kids. But she's here in spirit."

Rachel opened her mouth to speak, then couldn't when her throat got tight and her eyes began to burn.

"You didn't have to do this," she managed to say, "but I'm really glad you did."

Nina exhaled in obvious relief. "Here I was all braced to be told to mind my own business. I'm glad you're not mad." She slipped an arm around Rachel. "All right. Let's go talk to this doctor. Between us, we've had a lot of kids and we know the right questions to ask. You'll be fine. Pregnancy is sometimes easy, sometimes hard, but then you have a baby and it's all worth it."

"She's right," Liz said, claiming her other arm. "When you're ready, we'll tell you stories about childbirth. It's not so bad."

"Take the drugs," Merry added.

"Exactly," Liz said with a grin. "Why suffer?"

They continued to offer advice all through the elevator ride and into the doctor's office. The four of them claimed a corner of the cheerful waiting room. Rachel held on to Nina's hand and found she didn't miss her own mother quite so much.

"This means a lot to me," she said. "You can't know how much."

"We're happy to be here." Nina patted her hand. "This isn't about Carter, you know. This is about you. Whatever happens with him, you're one of the family."

Rachel touched her stomach. The pregnancy had been an accident and for a while she'd thought it might be a disaster, but now she was starting to wonder if having this child was the best thing that had ever happened to her.

"Dr. Richards will see you now," the nurse said. "She'd like you to start in her office, so you can talk. She'll do the exam after."

They rose together and headed for the large office. There were plenty of chairs. Nina stayed next to Rachel while Merry and Liz were on either side of them.

When Dr. Richards entered, she grinned. "I love it when a baby brings a family together. Good afternoon, ladies."

Rachel bit her lower lip. "I know this is kind of a lot but…"

Her doctor, an attractive woman in her mid-forties, shook her head. "Don't apologize. The more support, the better. There's no better source of information for a pregnant woman than other women who have been through it already. They understand what's happening to your body and they know what questions to ask. All right, first things first. Your due date."

Rachel fought against embarrassment as she said, "I, um, know the day I got pregnant."

Liz nudged her. "I heard it was night."

Merry laughed. "I heard it was a very good night."

"Girls," Nina scolded. "Stop. You'll upset Rachel."

But Rachel didn't mind the teasing. It made her feel a little less self-conscious.

"Technically it was night," she admitted and gave the date.

"That makes the calculations easier," Dr. Richards told her. "So we have a due date."

"Not that the baby will come that day," Nina said.

"Exactly," Dr. Richards said. "But it gives us something to shoot for. I'll be giving you an examination and doing some preliminary blood work. I expect everything to go normally. You're in great health. There are some dietary changes I'd like you to make, which we'll also discuss."

"Prenatal vitamins," Liz said with a groan. "They made me constipated, so drink lots of water."

"Yeah, drink now, before the baby decides to spend all day sitting on your bladder."

They continued talking, exchanging stories and advice. Rachel listened more to their voices than their words. The information wasn't as important to her as the connection. They had meant what they said—that she was one of them now. A member of the family. It had been so very long since she'd been able to be a part of something so very precious.

Carter stopped by his mother's house after work.

"You called?" he said as he walked into the kitchen and found her stirring something on the stove.

She raised her head for his kiss, then studied him with her dark eyes. "I wanted to talk to you."

"Water heater working all right?" he asked as he grabbed a cookie from the cooling rack and then pulled out a chair at the round table by the bay window.

"It's fine. You're always good to me, Carter. You come by whenever I need you. You're the same with your sisters."

He wasn't sure he liked the sound of that. On the surface, it seemed to be a compliment, but he knew his mother and she hadn't asked him to stop by so she could give him a pat on the back. Life was never that easy.

"And?" he prompted.

"You're a good man. I appreciate that. I take some of the credit."

He grinned. "Of course you do."

Her smile faded. "Rachel went to the doctor today."

He dropped the cookie onto the table and stood. "What? Is she all right? Did anything happen?"

His mother waved him back into his chair. "She's fine. It was a routine prenatal visit."

Right—pregnant women had to go to the doctor. That made sense. "She didn't tell me," he said, more to himself than his mother. He'd seen Rachel most of the weekend. Why hadn't she said anything to him? Was she trying to keep him from getting too involved or had she thought he wouldn't be interested?

Whatever she thought of him, he had a right to be involved. He was the baby's father.

"She didn't tell anyone," his mother said. "I saw the note when I was over on Saturday and Merry, Liz and I just showed up. I thought she might be angry, but she wasn't. Do you know why?"

"Because you bullied her and she didn't want to be rude?"

His mother narrowed her gaze. "Such a smart mouth. You didn't get that from me. No, she wasn't angry because she's alone, Carter. She's pregnant and alone in the world."

He actually knew that, but still, his mother's impressive ability to make him feel guilty kicked into play.

"I would have gone," he said. "I wanted to go. She never mentioned she was going to the doctor."

"Maybe you should ask. Your sisters have been pregnant enough for you to have an idea of what goes on. You have to get involved. There's going to be a baby soon, and then what?"

And then, he didn't know. The direction of this conversation was clear. He braced himself for the familiar attack, but instead of readying his arguments, he wondered if maybe his mother was right.

Whoa—where had that thought come from? Right?

"You should marry her," Nina said. "The baby will need a father, and don't tell me you're going to be a father regardless of whether or not you get married. You can't show up every other weekend, Carter. You need to be there all the time. You need to give this baby a name. Do the right thing. And not just because it's the right thing. Do it because you want to."

Marriage. He had very particular ideas about the institution—most of them involving him running as far and fast as he could. Sure, it looked good from the outside, but then what? How could he think about forever when he wasn't sure he believed he could ever be in love.

Except, for once, the idea wasn't so uncomfortable. He could see himself with Rachel in a few years. In a lot of years. He wouldn't mind fighting with her and making up with her. He kind of liked thinking about sharing diaper duty and decorating for Christmas. He suddenly wanted to know if she liked dogs.

Was he serious about this? Could he honestly imagine spending the rest of his life with Rachel? Fidelity had never been an issue, mostly because he always knew he could move on. But this time there would be no moving on. In his mind, marriage was forever.

Could he be with just her?

The answer came more easily than he ever could have imagined. Yes, he could be with her forever. He could grow old with her. He could love her.

Love? Him?

And if he could or did love her, what did she think about him? She'd been completely comfortable with the idea of not getting married. She was one of the few women he knew who *didn't* talk about getting married. Did that mean he'd finally found "the one" only to have her not want him? His ex-girlfriends would have a party in the streets if that turned out to be true.

But he was getting ahead of himself.

"Carter, are you listening to me?" his mother asked.

"Not really."

"Then listen to this. It's time for you to grow up."

A common theme in his life, he thought. First the captain and now her.

He stood and crossed to the stove. "Mama, I love you, but you don't get a say in this. I'll do anything for you except live my life the way you want me to. It's time for you to back off."

She eyed him. "You're standing up to me."

"It's not the first time."

"I know, but I think maybe now you mean it."

"I do."

She smiled. "You're a good man, Carter. I'm very proud of you."

He kissed her again and left. As he crossed the street to his own house, he was again reminded that there were way too many women in his world. Was he really thinking of inviting in one more?

Chapter Eleven

Rachel pushed her cart through the grocery store. Carter had called and suggested barbecuing that night. He'd offered to bring everything, including a portable grill, but she'd insisted on providing dinner. After all, their last couple of meals had been compliments of him…or at least his family.

Carter being a typical guy, she bypassed chicken in favor of steaks, then picked up some ingredients for salad. In the dairy aisle, she grabbed a few cartons of yogurt to help with her calcium intake.

It felt strange to be shopping for two—in a guy way, not a baby way—and yet it was fun. She'd been alone for a long time and having Carter around was nice. More than nice. He was a lot of things she'd been looking for in a man. So was she being too hasty in thinking they couldn't maybe work things out?

The biggest problem was how Carter saw her. Was she someone he would get serious about? Was he—

"Hi. I know this is really weird, but are you Rachel?"

Rachel turned to see a stunning blonde in a T-shirt tight enough to cut off circulation smiling at her. Describing the woman as "pretty" was practically an insult. She defined beautiful, from her gleaming, waist-length hair to her large blue eyes.

"What?" Rachel blinked and tried to get her brain to work.

The woman smiled. That was perfect, too. "I'm sorry. I'm Pam. Liz and I go way back. She mentioned you were seeing Carter. My two kids go to your school, so I've seen you around. How is he?"

Carter had dated this…this…goddess?

"I, ah, he's fine," Rachel said, knowing she sounded about as stupid and clueless as she felt. Suddenly her sensible dress seemed drab and unflattering. Her makeup had long since worn off, although there weren't enough skin products in the world to get her face to look like Pam's.

Pam's smile widened. "I fell for Carter when I was seventeen. And eighteen and nineteen. We were young and things were a little volatile. Liz is thrilled he's finally found the one. I'm totally content in my life, but I'll admit to a twinge of envy when I heard he was settling down. Carter's one of the good guys. I hope you two are really happy."

The other woman's sincere good wishes made Rachel feel like slime, especially since she and Carter were still in the pretend dating stage of their relationship.

"Thanks," she murmured as Pam moved away.

Later, when Rachel had carried the groceries into her apartment and set them on the counter, she stared out the window. The women were everywhere. How many had he dated? A hundred? Five hundred? She supposed that logically all that one-on-one interaction would mean that he would be completely clear on who and what he wanted. While he'd never indicated she was that one, if she was, could she handle it? Could she give her heart knowing that for the next ten or fifteen years women would be coming up to him and offering various degrees of good wishes, some sincerely, some wishing they were in her place?

She didn't have an answer, she just knew the question made her uncomfortable and she wasn't sure why.

An hour later she'd changed into a flirty skirt and a sleeveless T-shirt in what she refused to believe was any kind of attempt to compete with Pam. That relationship had been over for years, right? Carter probably didn't even remember her.

But when he arrived, barbecue and all, she invited him inside, then mentioned running into Pam in the grocery store.

He kissed her lightly, then smiled. "I haven't seen Pam in a while. How is she?"

Not exactly the "Pam who?" she'd been hoping for.

"Fine. Gorgeous. She mentioned she was friends with Liz."

He nodded. "They were always tight. Pam is my age, a couple of years younger than Liz, but she'd skipped a few grades in school, so they were in the same high school class."

Rachel held in a groan. Beautiful *and* brilliant? Was that fair?

"She seemed very nice."

"She is," he told her. "So are you. How was your day?"

"Fine." Other than the Pam encounter.

"I haven't seen you in a couple of days. How was your doctor's appointment?"

The change in subject caught her off guard. She'd planned on more Pam talk, but the doctor was a good subject, too.

"Great. I was really nervous about going. I don't know why. I've been seeing Dr. Richards since I moved here. She's great. Very approachable and patient. I'm glad she'll be delivering my baby. But this is the first time I'm pregnant, so I didn't know what to expect. Your mom and sisters showed up." She frowned. "But if you're asking about the appointment, I guess you already know that."

"Were you angry they were there?"

"Not at all. I appreciated the support. It was weird— as I was driving there, I was missing my mom. I know it's been a long time since she died, but sometimes I feel like I won't make it if I can't talk to her one more time. Seeing your family there really helped."

She paused and waited for him to say something or at least nod. Instead she couldn't figure out his expression and he seemed almost…angry.

"Carter, if I don't mind that they came, then you shouldn't," she told him.

His eyes darkened. "That's not the point. This is my baby, too. You didn't mention the doctor's appointment to me. I told you I wanted to be a part of things. This is important to me, Rachel. I don't want you shutting me out."

She opened her mouth, then closed it. Guilt and shame settled in the pit of her stomach.

"I'm sorry," she told him, meaning it. "I really never thought…"

He stiffened. "Thought what?"

She swallowed. "That you'd be interested," she whispered.

Nothing about him changed, but she had the feeling that she'd just cut him deeply. Funny how until this moment, she'd never considered that Carter had feelings like everyone else. He was always so charming and in charge of every situation.

She reached for his hand, then pulled back. Touching didn't seem like a good idea.

"I was wrong," she said, gazing directly at him. "Totally wrong. I should have told you about the appointment. I wasn't deliberately trying to shut you out. It won't happen again. I'll let you know every time I see the doctor. I promise."

Carter nodded. He was still pissed, but didn't feel he

had the right anymore. Rachel had admitted the mistake and said she wouldn't repeat it. He should let it go.

The thing was, he didn't want to. He wasn't sure why this got to him, but it did.

"I mean it," she told him. "I am sorry."

"I know you are. You don't have to keep saying that."

"You're still upset."

He consciously relaxed. "I'm a guy. We don't get upset."

One corner of her mouth twitched. "Crabby, then. You're a little crabby and moody."

He growled low in his throat and she laughed. Her hand settled on his arm.

"Seriously," she said. "I'm sorry. It won't happen again."

"I know. I'm fine. Let's change the subject."

She hesitated, then tugged him over the sofa. "How was your day?"

"Good. We're getting close to making the bust."

"Will that be dangerous?"

"Not especially."

"Why don't I believe you?" she asked.

"Not a clue."

In truth, there was always a risk, but it was minor and he didn't want to worry her.

"Then what?" she asked. "Do you take another undercover assignment?"

"Maybe." He hadn't decided. "You hungry? I can set up the grill."

"Sure. I cleared a spot on the back balcony. I didn't

think it would be a good idea for my plants to go up in flames."

Nearly an hour later, dinner was prepared. He brought in the steaks, while she served salad and baked potatoes.

She moved with an easy grace that made him think of other things she did well. But instead of getting lost in his ever-present passion, he pushed his need away. There were different things they had to deal with and this seemed to be as good a time as any.

"Tell me about the guys you were engaged to before," he said.

She froze in the act of passing him salad dressing. "Excuse me?"

Okay, maybe not his smoothest transition, but he'd been thinking about her previous engagements. "I've been wondering what went wrong," he admitted. "You wouldn't have agreed to marry them in the first place if they'd been jerks."

She passed over the bottle of ranch dressing and gave him a smile that didn't reach her eyes. "Thanks for the support on that assumption," she said, her voice light but wary. "They weren't jerks. I realized I wasn't in love with either of them."

"Why?" he asked bluntly. "What changed? Was it them? Was it you?"

She picked up her fork, then set it down. "I'm not sure who changed. With Brett, we were both young. We'd met our freshman year, sort of clinging to each other for support. Neither of us had dated much before that. We started out as friends and things progressed from there. After a while the relationship turned serious."

"So he proposed?"

She nodded slowly. "I was kind of surprised, actually. But in a good way. He was nice and sweet and I thought…" She shrugged. "I thought I was in love with him."

Carter wasn't excited to hear about the other men in her life, but he knew the information was important.

"What changed your mind?" he asked.

"I just wasn't. I still cared about him, but not in a romantic way. I realized that for me the relationship hadn't really gone past friendship. I'd been excited by the thought of a serious boyfriend, but I hadn't considered that Brett wasn't the right guy for me."

Logical, he thought. He almost believed her. "And the other one?"

"This isn't exactly dinner conversation," she told him.

"I don't mind, if you don't."

He suspected she wanted to say she did mind, but couldn't figure out how.

"Okay. Well, I met Ray in my senior year of college. I was a student teaching a couple of days a week and he was a teacher at the same school. We were a lot alike. He was great with kids and funny and really smart. He was getting his Ph.D. in education at night and planned on becoming a principal."

Carter hated the guy immediately. "So what happened?"

Rachel sighed. "The usual. He asked me out, I accepted and things progressed fairly quickly. I fell in love with him. He proposed, I said yes, we set a date."

His muscles clenched. "And?"

"And I couldn't imagine myself married to him. There was nothing wrong with him. I was the problem. I broke things off and returned the ring." She looked at him. "I'm sorry this isn't more dramatic. If I'd known I was supposed to provide entertainment during dinner, I would have planned better stories."

He'd annoyed her, but that was the least of his problems. "You don't let people in," he said.

She stared at him. "Excuse me? I tell you about two relationships and you're ready to make a judgment on my character?"

"It's not a judgment. I'm stating a fact. You don't let people get close."

She put her napkin on the table and glared at him. "At least I can count the number of relationships I've had without having to get out a calculator. If you want to talk about people who aren't willing to take that next step, maybe you should look in the mirror."

"I didn't believe in the next step," he said. "You did. You wanted to get married and have kids. You wanted normal. So why did you agree to marry two different guys only to back out when it all got too real?"

She stood. "Let me guess. You're going to tell me everything that's wrong with me. How helpful. I should probably listen. After all, you have plenty of experience with women."

He'd hurt her, which he hadn't meant to do. He rose. "Rachel, stop. I'm not saying this to upset you. I'm trying to understand. You're an incredible woman. I've seen you with the kids in your class. You're warm and caring and they adore you. So why aren't you married? Why weren't either of those other guys the one?"

"You tell me," she said tightly.

Damn. He hadn't wanted the conversation to go this way. But now that it had... "You don't let people in. Your friends, my family, even me, we only get so far."

"You don't know what you're talking about," she told him. "Maybe I don't let you in because I don't want to. Based on your track record, you're not exactly a good bet in the romance department. Besides, this isn't real. Those were your rules. Pretend dating so we could break up later. I find it interesting that you weren't willing to get to know the woman having your child."

"I was interested," he told her, doing his best to stay focused and logical. "You came to me with papers for me to sign giving up the rights to my kid. You made it clear from the start that you weren't in this for anything but the baby."

"Right. So you're saying that otherwise, you would have tried to make things work with me?"

"Yes."

She rolled her eyes. "I don't believe you. You've made a career out of not committing. At least I've tried."

"What makes you think I haven't? Because I haven't gotten engaged and then changed my mind? Is that the measure of a real commitment? Because if that's what you want, let's do it. We'll get engaged. Then you can break up with me later because you've changed your mind."

He knew he'd gone too far even before she paled and then pointed to the door.

"Get out," she said, her voice low and trembling.

He stalked across the room, then turned. "You never gave me a chance," he said. "Why was that? We have great chemistry, we get along. Is it my job? Is it my past? Or is it you? We're having a baby together, Rachel. Shouldn't you be trying?"

"I am trying," she yelled. "What do you want from me? We've played all of this by your rules and now I'm in trouble because of that? Here's a news flash—I don't have to be married to have a baby. I'm fine on my own. I'm comfortable being a single parent. I'm sorry if that doesn't satisfy your fantasy, but I can't be responsible for that."

He frowned. "I thought you said you wanted a family. Husband, kids, the whole thing. Did I imagine that?"

She paused. "No. I'd always thought… Dammit, Carter, stop doing this."

He'd never heard her swear before. "You say you want it all, but you don't act like it. The way things have happened in your past tell me that you're the one in the way of the dream, not me. I stand by what I said before. You don't let anyone get inside. You might want to think about why that is."

* * *

Rachel hadn't slept much that night. She'd had big plans for a wonderful evening and Carter had ruined them with his stupid accusations.

What was up with him? Who did he think he was? He didn't know her well enough to be critical of her or her choices. It wasn't as if he'd lived *his* life perfectly.

She was a good person and a good friend. She'd always worked hard to do the right thing. So why had he jumped all over her? Was it his ego talking because she refused to be one of a crowd? Couldn't he stand the thought that there was one woman who didn't desperately want to be with him?

But as she drove across town after work, she found that making him the bad guy didn't make her feel any better. She'd hated fighting with him and she'd been unable to forget some of what he'd said. Like the part about not letting people in. That wasn't true. She had lots of close, intimate relationships. Why did he have to think the worst of her and why did she care?

She pulled into the parking lot and walked toward the large entrance to the all-woman workout center. Crissy owned four gyms in the area. This was the biggest, with her company offices on the second floor.

"Is she in?" Rachel asked Crissy's assistant, then gave her name.

After being buzzed, her friend walked out to greet her. "Hey, you. This is unexpected. What's up?"

Rachel clutched her purse in both hands. "I need to talk. Is this a good time?"

"Absolutely."

After asking her assistant to hold all calls, Crissy led Rachel into her bright and spacious office. When they were settled on the sofa, Crissy turned to her.

"I'm feeling especially nonjudgmental today," Crissy said with a warm smile. "Tell me everything."

Now that she was here, Rachel wasn't sure how to start. Maybe with last night. "Carter and I had a fight and I hate that. He was unfair and difficult and I'm not sure what he wanted, but he really bugged me."

"He's a guy. Sometimes they can't help it."

"I know, but this was different. He wanted to know about the other guys in my life. The two men I was engaged to. I thought it was a weird topic, but I gave him the five-minute version of what happened. Then he said the reason things hadn't worked out is that I'm not emotionally accessible. Can you believe it? Me? He was talking to me like I was some kind of scary loner. There's nothing wrong with me."

Crissy patted her arm. "Of course there isn't. Look, I don't know what Carter's problem is. Maybe he was threatened by your past."

"Oh, please. The man has dated thousands of women. I'm just one in a long line."

"Then he has other issues. Everyone has different emotional boundaries. Didn't you say that his family is running in and out of his place all the time? That sounds a little flaky. He's kind of a mama's boy, isn't he? And just a little too close to his sisters. If you ask me, he's the one with the issues."

Rachel drew in a breath. She'd come to her friend for a shoulder to cry on, not to get into a fight. "Carter isn't a mama's boy. That's not really fair. He's a great guy. Very responsible. Sure, he cares about his family, but he's also willing to put his life on the line in his job. He's a good guy. Trustworthy and honest and…"

She saw the corners of Crissy's mouth twitch, as if her friend were holding in a smile.

"At least we know you like him," Crissy said. "I wanted to be sure."

Rachel sighed. "You set me up."

"Just a little. If you hated the guy, that would change my advice."

"I don't hate him, but he's impossible. I think he expects me to fall at his feet and that's not going to happen."

"I agree. That whole feet-falling never really helps anyone. But I do have a question. If he is, as you said, a good guy, then why didn't you ever consider marrying him? You're having a child together and marrying the baby's father remains the traditional response."

"For one thing, he made it clear he didn't want to marry me. Why would I pursue him?"

"Okay. But if he doesn't want to marry you and you don't want to marry him, why do you care what he thinks about you? If he's wrong about you, so what?"

Rachel opened her mouth then closed it. "Good point," she said slowly. "I don't know why I care, but I do. I hated what he said."

"So his comment about not letting people in pushed a button for you."

"Maybe." Rachel drew in a deep breath. "Yes. It bugged me big-time."

"Why?"

"I'm not like that."

"So he was wrong."

"Yes. Maybe." Rachel leaned back against the sofa and closed her eyes. "I guess, maybe, he's not totally wrong. I sometimes think it hurts too much to care. You know, because I lost my family when I was so young."

She opened her eyes and saw Crissy looking at her.

"Are you upset because he saw the truth or because he articulated something you're not proud of?" her friend asked.

"Both, I think. I know I never want to feel that pain again. It was so horrible. I kept thinking that if I could die, too, everything would be all right."

Long dormant emotions tried to surge to life, but Rachel suppressed them with a skill born of years of practice. No way she wanted to go there. Not now. Not ever.

"So you're holding back to protect yourself," Crissy said. "That makes sense. For you, the price of belonging isn't worth the risk. We all make trade-offs."

Rachel wasn't sure she liked the sound of that. "I belong."

"Where?" Crissy asked gently. "I'm not judging you, honey. I'm the last person to do that. I'm just saying, are you sure you're where you want to be? Are you acting or reacting? The past can be powerful and an influence we can't shake."

Rachel had never thought about not having a choice. "I didn't want to marry Brett or Ray. I wasn't willing to go through with it just to prove a point."

"Good for you," Crissy told her. "Are you avoiding a relationship with Carter because he's not the one or because you're afraid?"

"I don't love him," Rachel said stubbornly. "Just because I can list all his good qualities doesn't make him Mr. Right."

"What does it make him?"

Rachel didn't have an answer for that. Just as difficult, deep in her heart, she wasn't sure what she felt for Carter. "Everything is so confusing."

"Life always is."

Rachel shook her head. "Not for you. You're the most together person I know."

Crissy didn't smile. "I'm faking it as much as anyone else." She shrugged. "Okay, here's my confession. I'm nearly thirty. I've never been married. Despite what I say about hating first dates, there have been plenty of great guys. So why didn't I pick one of them?"

Rachel had never much thought about her friend's personal life. "Why didn't you?" she asked.

"Because I can't. I'm not allowed. My punishment is to never fall in love, never be romantically happy, never have a child."

"That's crazy," Rachel breathed. "Why would you think that? You don't have to be punished."

"Actually, I do." Crissy drew in a deep breath. "I got pregnant in high school. It was my senior year. I didn't mean for it to happen, but then who does? I didn't want to marry the guy and he didn't want a kid. I found out I didn't, either. So I took the easy way out. I gave up my baby."

She stood and crossed to the window. There she folded her arms over her chest. "I could have kept him. My parents were supportive and offered to help. But I wasn't interested. I knew a child would tie me down. A child would change everything, and I didn't want that. I had dreams. The irony is I gave him up without a second thought and ever since, I've been unable to let him go."

Rachel rose and joined her friend. "You've been thinking about your son?"

Crissy nodded. "It's been getting worse. Maybe because I'm nearly thirty and I can hear rumblings from my biological clock. Maybe the guilt is growing. I don't know. He's twelve. The family is local, even. They send me pictures and letters. He's a good kid. Happy. I couldn't have done as decent a job."

Rachel didn't know what to say. She couldn't believe Crissy had carried this secret for so long. "Do you want to meet him?"

"I don't know," her friend admitted. "I have a standing invitation to come on by whenever I'd like. But what do I say? 'I'm the woman who couldn't be bothered?' There's a statement."

"You were only eighteen," Rachel reminded her. "You were in high school."

"I was lazy. I did what was easy, but I don't know if it was right. Now there's no going back. Even if I go meet him, I will never be what I could have been. I will never be more than the woman who gave birth to him. Someone else is his mother."

Crissy turned and looked at Rachel. "You can't imagine what this is like. I can't know what you went through when you lost your family. It was horrible and you will always feel that pain. But you do need to figure out how it impacts you today. If you don't care about Carter, if he's just some fun guy you messed up with, then great. But if he could be more, then you need to think about that. You've always talked about wanting a family. You've always said that was important to you and I think it is. There are a lot of good men out there, but it would be so much easier if you could fall for your baby's father."

Rachel nodded slowly. "I have to figure out why I'm avoiding him."

"I would. This is a big deal. This is the rest of your life."

She hugged Crissy. "I'm sorry about what happened to you. I wish I could make it better."

"It's okay. All of this is my responsibility. I can handle it."

"You shouldn't have to handle it alone. If you want to talk, or decide to go meet him, I'm happy to be there. Really."

"I appreciate that. Right now I'm not doing anything."

Rachel managed a smile. "That's kind of how I feel."

Crissy touched Rachel's stomach. "I have time on my side. You don't. There's going to be a baby before you know it. Trust me, they change everything. Even when you don't keep them."

Rachel nodded. She knew her friend was right. A baby *would* change everything. The question was what would she do about it?

Carter or not Carter. What did he want from her? Just as important, what did she want from him?

Chapter Twelve

Rachel paced her apartment restlessly. Normally she loved a day off midweek. It was unexpected and she always felt so decadent sleeping in when she would normally be rushing around to get ready. But despite the time off work, today she felt out of sorts and jumpy. She couldn't settle in to any one task. It was time to do some serious pruning on her plants and even that didn't excite her.

It was all because she hadn't talked to Carter in nearly a week, she thought grimly. She'd picked up the phone about fifty times, but hadn't made the call. Partly because she wanted him to come to her and partly because she didn't know what to say.

He'd been wrong about her. Totally and completely wrong. Absolutely wrong and maybe just a little right.

She stalked out onto her back balcony and started plucking off dead flowers. "So I don't embrace the world with open arms," she muttered. "He does that enough for any five people. I care. I have friends. I know how to love. I…"

Love. Somehow the word got stuck in her brain. She believed in love. She desperately wanted to be *in* love. She wanted to feel safe and cared for and as if she finally belonged. She wanted to be home.

But the thought of loving and being loved and depending on that love terrified her. Loving meant losing and that was so not for her.

Rachel straightened. What did that mean? That she was letting fear rule her life?

"Of course not," she muttered. "I'm being careful and sensible, which does not define Carter."

He was all things wild, which made him exciting in bed, but what about in the real world? Did she want that kind of uncertainty every day? She still believed he'd set her up—establishing ground rules and then punishing her for following them. But if they were both wrong then neither of them could be right. She really hated that.

With her plants plucked, she returned to her apartment and glanced at the to-do list she'd prepared for herself. Nothing sounded very exciting, but folding laundry was a must. She cleared the coffee table, dumped everything on the sofa, then flipped on the TV to keep her company.

But instead of a morning talk show, she found herself staring at a helicopter shot of a street. A familiar street.

"This is live coverage of a standoff in Riverside. The police spokesman tells us that their raid on a motorcycle repair shop went bad when suspects opened fire. Two people have been shot, although they are still trapped inside. Until suspects release them, they will be unable to receive medical attention."

The reporter kept talking, but Rachel wasn't listening. She recognized the building in the center of the television as the one where Carter was working. Which meant he was inside. Had they found out he was an undercover cop?

Panic gripped her. Panic and fear. She lunged for the phone and started to dial his cell only to hang up mid-number. She couldn't phone him. She had no idea what was happening. If the phone rang at the wrong time, it could get him killed.

Now what? Her thoughts whirled frantically. Her chest hurt and she had trouble breathing. Now what?

Not knowing what else to do, she grabbed her purse and her car keys, then hurried downstairs. Fifteen minutes later, she pulled up in front of Carter's mother's house. After the fight she'd had with Carter, she wasn't sure how she would be welcomed.

Shelly answered her knock.

"I was worried," Rachel said by way of explanation.

"Of course you were. We all are."

"Is it okay that I'm here?"

Shelly smiled. "You're family, Rachel. Where else would you go?"

Some of the fear was replaced by relief. Until that moment, she hadn't realized how much she'd been worried about everyone hating her for arguing with Carter. But based on Shelly's reaction, she wondered if they even knew there'd been a falling out.

But if their plan had been to pretend date and then have a pretend fight for the sake of his relatives, why hadn't he told them about the real disagreement?

Shelly ushered her into the family room at the back of the house. Nina was sitting on the sofa with Liz and Merry on either side of her. The TV was on the same channel as Rachel's had been. When the older woman saw her, she stood and embraced her.

"We talked about calling you," Nina said as she clutched Rachel's arms. "I thought you'd be at work. You're not teaching today?"

Rachel shook her head. "No. It's one of those weird holidays where only schools close. When I saw what had happened, I didn't know what to do, so I came here. I hope you don't mind."

"Of course not," Merry said, scooting over to make room on the couch. "We're all worried. Of course Carter is going to be all right, but until we know for sure…"

Her voice trailed off. Rachel understood. She felt exactly the same way. Of course Carter was fine. How could he be anything but? Still, until she knew for sure, it was difficult to think about anything else.

Liz jumped to her feet. "I'm going to get something to drink. Is there coffee, Mama? Should I make a pot?"

"You can make some more," Nina told her.

"Rachel, I have herbal tea. Would you like that? To soothe you?"

Rachel didn't think tea would help, but she sensed Liz wanted to be doing something. "That would be nice. Thank you."

"I'll help," Shelly said and joined her sister in the kitchen.

Merry clutched her mother's hand. "I can't stand this," she whispered. "The only thing worse than Carter being there would be Adam inside, too."

"Until we know better, we assume the best," Nina said firmly, even as she stroked her daughter's short, dark hair. "Carter knows what he's doing. He's smart and capable. He's good at his job. How many people are in the building? Ten? Twenty? He's not one of the ones who was shot. You'll see. And if he is, he's strong. He'll pull through. He has Rachel and the baby to live for."

Nina held out her free hand and Rachel took it. As their fingers clutched tightly, she felt both the older woman's emotional strength and her own guilt.

Carter didn't have her to live for. Even though she hadn't intentionally kept him out of the loop with the baby, that was how he felt. So he didn't have that, either.

She told herself that Carter was a tough guy and that she wouldn't make or break his survival. But still, she worried.

The women sat together for several hours. The standoff continued. Rachel forced herself to nibble on a sandwich for the sake of the baby, even though every bite made her want to throw up. Nina stayed strong.

Only the trembling in her fingers betrayed her worry. Merry, Liz and Shelly clung to each other and promised that Carter would be fine.

Shortly after one in the afternoon, someone shot tear gas into the building. Several police officers stormed inside and there was the sound of gunshots. Rachel's breath caught in her throat. She couldn't stand watching this, but not knowing was worse. Carter, she prayed desperately. Please let Carter be all right.

Twenty minutes later, the worst was over. Paramedics rushed in and three men were brought out on stretchers. The women crowded around the television, trying to see if one of them was Carter. Suddenly the phone rang.

Nina rushed to grab it.

Merry clutched Rachel's arm. "They'll let us know either way," she whispered. "If he's been hurt, his captain will call. If he's all right, he'll call."

Merry's fingers dug into Rachel's skin, but she didn't pull back. She waited and prayed until Nina said, "Carter, is that you?"

There was silence, then Nina sank into a chair and began to cry. She held up her hand and nodded through the tears.

"He's fine," she mouthed. "He's fine."

Rachel and Merry embraced, while Shelly and Liz did the same. Then they huddled in a heartfelt group hug as Rachel felt her tension begin to ease.

"It's hard," Liz told her, wiping away her own tears. "Knowing Frank risks his life every day is so hard, but I get through it. We all do. We have each other and you have us."

Rachel touched her face and was surprised to find her cheeks damp. Apparently she'd given in to tears, too.

"We stay strong for each other," Shelly said.

"I can see that." Rachel's throat was still tight, so it hurt to speak.

These women kept each other going. She envied the connection they had and how they were there for each other. She'd always wanted that.

Nina hung up the phone. "He's fine. He had to go help with the arrests and give a statement. There will be paperwork."

Her daughters groaned. "There's always paperwork," Merry said. "You get used to it."

Nina smiled at Rachel. "You get used to all of it. Would I have liked Carter's father to be in a less dangerous line of work? Of course. But he was who he was. I didn't want to change him. So you pray, you keep busy, you love while you can."

Rachel nodded. It made sense and in a perfect world, that was what would happen. But her problems with Carter weren't about his job. They were about so much more.

"I should get going," she said. "I'm so glad he's fine."

Nina hugged her. "He's a good man, my Carter."

"Yes, he is. One of the best."

That much was true. Carter's goodness wasn't in question. Instead, she had to wonder about her feelings and his feelings and what each of them wanted and when their rules of pretend dating had suddenly changed.

* * *

Carter finished up his paperwork at about eight that night. He was exhausted, but it had been a day he'd worked hard for and it had come out right. The bad guys were in jail or the hospital, the good guys were safe and he was damn proud to be a cop.

He drove home and parked in his driveway, but instead of going inside, he crossed the street and knocked on his mother's door. He wasn't going to stay, but she'd insisted on seeing him that night, swearing she wouldn't sleep until she knew for herself that he was fine.

She opened the door and instead of speaking, she just pulled him close.

He held her awkwardly, feeling how small she was and knowing he'd put her through hell that day.

"I'm fine," he murmured.

"Of course you are. Why wouldn't you be? You were just doing your job. Still, when the bullets go flying, a mother has a right to worry."

"You're good at that."

She stepped back and smiled at him. "I've had practice. We all have."

"The girls were here?"

Dumb question, he thought. Once word spread, all three of his sisters would end up here.

"And Rachel," his mother said. "She saw the standoff live on TV and came over. I'm glad she did. A time like this, a woman needs her family around her."

"Rachel was here?"

"Where else would she go?"

Interesting question, he thought. He'd wondered about her. But they hadn't talked in a while and he'd figured she was still mad at him.

"She was worried," his mother said, poking him in the chest. "And in her condition, she shouldn't have to worry so much."

"I know. So, um, she left?"

"After you'd called to say you were safe. You haven't talked?"

He shook his head.

His mother pushed him out the door. "So go. Call. Be with her. She was frantic, Carter. This kind of thing is hard for all of us, but for Rachel it's also new. Go show her you're fine."

"Thanks, Mama," he said. "I love you."

She smiled. "I love you, too. You make me very proud."

He stepped off the porch and headed back to his place.

So Rachel had been at his mother's. What did that mean? Had her fear been bigger than her anger? Should he call? Go by? He swore under his breath and opened his front door.

He hated not knowing what to do next, mostly because it never happened to him. He always knew. Getting involved was easy. Only this time it wasn't. This time it was complicated in ways he couldn't understand.

He flipped on the light by the door then came to a stop when he saw Rachel curled up on his sofa. Goldie lay at the other end, her head on Rachel's thigh.

Rachel opened her eyes and smiled at him. "Hey. Liz showed me where you kept the spare key, so I let myself in. I fed Goldie and decided to just wait. I wanted to see if you were okay."

"I'm fine."

"I can see that." She pushed herself into a sitting position and lowered her bare feet to the floor. "I thought you might call."

"I didn't know if you wanted to hear from me."

Her green eyes were bright with emotion. "I did. Despite everything, I wanted to talk to you."

Which told him what? That she'd been worried? Okay, worry was nice, but it wasn't exactly what he was looking for.

"So talk."

He lowered himself into the club chair opposite the sofa. Goldie wagged her tail but didn't stir from her comfy place on the couch.

"Were you scared?" she asked.

Not exactly the subject he'd thought she'd bring up but if she needed to stall for a few minutes, he could respect that.

"Not really," he told her. "No one in the shop thought I was a cop, so I was safe from them. An overeager shooter could have taken me out, but I figured the odds of that were slim. It was a waiting game."

"I was terrified. So was your mom and your sisters. We knew people had been injured, but we didn't know if it was you."

He raised both hands, then glanced down at his chest. "I'm good."

She shifted so she could stroke Goldie's head. "You

didn't tell them about our fight. I thought you might, so I wasn't sure if I would be welcome." She glanced at him. "I thought you were looking for a chance for our pretend dating to end. Why didn't you take it?"

"I didn't think of it," he told her honestly. He'd been angry about what had happened, and confused, but he'd never thought to tell anyone else about it.

Her eyes widened slightly. "Okay. I'll go with that. But you set me up, Carter. You established the rules, then got mad because I followed them."

He'd known they would get around to this eventually. "Maybe," he admitted, hating that he had to. "But I made up the rules because of how you started things."

"I didn't know you," she protested. "I never thought you'd be interested in having a baby with me."

"Maybe you should have gotten to know me before you assumed I was some jerk who would walk away from his kid."

She pressed her lips together, then nodded. "You're right. I found out I was pregnant and I freaked. Totally and completely. I guess I thought if there was no father, things would be easier."

"You want to do everything on your own?"

"Not really, but I wasn't very clear at the time."

"And now?" he asked.

"Now I know you're the kind of man who wants to be involved. And you will be."

He studied her. "Is that good or bad?"

She smiled. "Both."

He drew in a breath. "I didn't set you up. Not on

purpose. It just kind of happened. We had rules in place and you didn't mind them."

"Did you?" she asked, her voice sounding a little breathless.

"Some. I don't know what I feel, Rachel, but we're having a baby. I think our daughter deserves more than a halfhearted attempt to get to know each other. I think she deserves some serious effort."

"You don't know we're having a girl."

"Yeah, I do. It's the one thing I'm very clear on."

"I hope I have a boy just to shock you."

He smiled. "I'd like that."

She leaned toward him. "What do you want?"

Right that minute, he wanted her. In his arms, in his bed, under him, naked. He wanted to touch her and feel her. He wanted to close his eyes and go to sleep knowing she was there.

But that wasn't what she was talking about. She meant what did he want in the big-picture sense. As in for more than today.

He stiffened as he realized his answer was the same. He wanted Rachel in his life. He wanted to wake up and have her next to him.

The truth was a bitch, he thought, not sure what to do with the information. He'd never been the guy who did long term, so why was he thinking about it now? Why her? Was it because they were having a baby together?

He shook his head. No, this was bigger than that.

"Carter? The question wasn't supposed to be that hard."

"I want us to try," he said. "I want us to think about making it real."

He wanted to say a whole lot more, but a warning voice told him if he pushed too hard too fast he would scare Rachel away. He still believed she held back, that strong emotion scared her and the last thing he wanted was for her to run.

She bit her lower lip. "Real as in really dating? Really getting involved?"

He nodded. "Can you handle that?"

She drew in a deep breath. "Yes, I can." She smiled. "Okay, I'm a little nervous, but I'll go with it."

He didn't want to give her too much time to think so he stood. After taking her hand, he pulled her to her feet and drew her close. "Nervous? Around me?"

"You're a big, tough guy," she said. "Dangerous."

"Very dangerous," he murmured, his mouth inches from hers. "Good in bed."

She sighed. "You're okay."

That made him grin. "Just okay."

She sniffed. "Some of your techniques need a little refining."

He saw the teasing light in her eyes and heard it in her voice.

"What kind of refining? Want to tell me?" He bent down and swept her up in his arms. "Or better yet, want to show me?"

Saturday morning Carter stepped out of the shower to find Rachel waiting for him in the bathroom. Since his bust had gone down the previous week, she'd been staying with him more than she'd been at home. He'd never lived with anyone before and he found he liked having her around.

One advantage of close, constant proximity was that they got to make love like regular people. Just last night they'd managed to get naked *and* talk before he'd had to claim her. Of course this morning they'd made love on the counter, while their waffles burned.

"Want to wash my back?" he asked as he reached for a towel. "I can get back in the shower."

"I'd love to but your mom called. She asked if we could bring ice to the barbecue because her ice maker is acting up."

"I'm not surprised," he said. "It's about a hundred years old. My sisters and I tried to buy her a new refrigerator for Christmas last year, but she found out and got mad. She said it was too much money. I explained split four ways, it's not that much, but she wouldn't listen. What?"

Rachel was smiling at him.

"I love listening to you talk about your family," she told him. "There's something warm in your voice. It makes me happy."

"Yeah?" Despite the fact that he was still wet and she'd showered and dressed earlier, he pulled her close. "You make me happy."

"I'm glad."

They kissed. The second her mouth pressed against his, wanting poured through him. The instant and natural reaction jabbed her in the leg.

"You are consistent," she said as she reached down and caressed him. "Normally I would totally agree, but we have to get ice and be there in half an hour."

"Tonight," he promised.

"Oh, yeah," she said as she stepped back. "Even if I have to force you."

She glanced down at his thigh, then frowned slightly. "I noticed that scar the first night we were together. It's so unusual. What happened?"

He finished drying off, then wrapped the towel around his waist. "I was being an idiot, climbing up on the back of the sofa to hang shoelaces over the curtain rod. I was maybe six. Mama kept telling me to stop, that I'd hurt myself, and I did. I fell through the window and sliced my leg open. I remember her telling me that if it had been a couple of inches north, I would have been hating life."

She winced. "I have to agree with her. I, for one, would have been deeply disappointed. Okay, big, bad guy. Go get dressed."

She strolled out of the bathroom. He watched her go. Rachel didn't seem to notice the changes in her body, but he could see them. Her breasts were fuller and, based on her recent ecstatic reactions to his touch, more sensitive. There was a slight curve to her stomach and thickening of her waist. She looked lush, like a woman coming in to her most beautiful time.

Carter was so used to feeling trapped and pressured in a relationship that he hadn't known what it was like to feel that everything was right. He belonged with

Rachel. She completed him and he wanted to be there for her. He wanted to hold her and support her and convince her that it was safe to care about him.

He wanted to love her.

Love. The one thing he never thought he would find. But he had. So what was he going to do about it?

After icing brownies, Rachel survived the water fight, then cuddled Liz's two girls as she dried them with a big towel in a sunny spot in the yard.

What a perfect day, she thought as the three of them sprawled on the grass and looked up at the clouds passing overhead.

"That one looks like Goldie," Erin, the youngest, said.

"I can see that," Rachel told her.

Around them the family laughed and talked. The guys had settled into a meaningful discussion about college bowl games, while the women kept an eye on the kids. Carter had ducked out about an hour ago and Rachel found herself listening for his arrival.

"Auntie Rachel, when I go to kindergarten next year, can I be in your class?" Erin asked.

Rachel ran her fingers through the little girl's silky hair. "I think you'll probably get Mrs. Reed for your teacher."

Erin pouted. "But I want to be in your class."

Rachel wasn't sure how to explain the complications of her having a child by Erin's uncle and how that would mean Erin would get a different teacher.

"Because I already know you and think you're so great, Mrs. Reed is going to want a chance to get to know you, too," she said. "I think you'll like her. She's a lot of fun. I'd want to be in her class."

Erin giggled. "You're too big and you're a teacher. You can't be in class."

A shadow fell across them.

"Uncle Carter!" Erin sat up and grinned. "You're back!"

"I am, Peanut." He held out a hand. "I'm going to steal Rachel away for a few minutes. Okay."

"Don't be long."

He chuckled. "I won't." He pulled Rachel to her feet.

"Where'd you run off to?" she asked. "I turned around and you were gone. Sneaking out on me?"

"Only now and then."

He led the way to the front of the house, then across to his place. Once they were inside, he faced her.

Rachel gazed into his handsome face and felt an instant quivering low in her stomach. Just being alone with the man was enough to make her want to have her way with him. But before she could move close and kiss him, he took her hands in his.

"I want to talk to you," he said, sounding serious.

"About?"

"A couple of things. I know how we met wasn't what either of us would have planned, and then you got pregnant, which complicated things. It was a giant twist of fate and for a long time I was kind of pissed off that my life wasn't in my control anymore."

She wasn't sure where he was going with this, but so far she agreed with him.

"I've never been a forever kind of guy," he continued. "I didn't get it. Other people fell in love and got married. Not me."

There was something wrong with her ears, she thought suddenly. A faint buzzing, as if she had a cold. And her skin was all tight. Go. She had to go.

"Carter," she began, but he shook his head.

"Let me finish."

She didn't need him to finish. He'd already said too much.

"I'm making this right," he told her. "Not because I have to but because it's what we both want. I love you, Rachel. I don't know how it happened, but I do. You're the one I want to be with forever. I want to learn everything about you. I want to share your hopes and dreams. I want us to make plans and have more kids and make a life. Just you. Only you."

He let go of her hands. Before she could run, he pulled a jewelry box out of his jeans pocket, then opened it. A beautiful solitaire diamond glimmered in the afternoon.

"It's taken me a long time to get here," he said, "but there's nowhere else I'd rather be. I love you, Rachel. Will you marry me?"

Chapter Thirteen

Rachel stared at the ring, then at Carter. Panic swept through her and with it, the need to run as far and as fast as she could. This was wrong. She didn't want to get married. Not to Carter. No. No! This wasn't happening. He couldn't be ruining everything like this.

"You're moving too fast," she said, barely able to catch her breath. The door beckoned, but she knew that she couldn't just bolt. Not without talking to him first.

"We're having a baby."

"I know, but marriage is not required."

Some of the light faded from his eyes. He closed the jewelry box. "You don't want to marry me," he said flatly.

"Carter, look. You're a great guy. You're practically

perfect. You're terrific. If I had to have a baby like this, you're the one I'd pick to do it with. But why change things? We have a good relationship. Let's not change that. We don't need the pressure."

She felt herself inching backward as she spoke. The door was so close, she thought frantically. If she could just get outside, then maybe she could breathe.

Carter couldn't believe this was happening. After all this time, after all the women he'd dated, the ones who had begged him to marry them, he'd finally fallen for the only one not interested in him that way. Here he was, ring in hand, heart exposed and from the looks of things, Rachel couldn't wait to get away from him.

Was it payback? A big cosmic joke on his behalf? Except he'd never led anyone on. He'd done his best to be honest.

Everything hurt. He'd been so sure that once Rachel knew how he felt about her, she'd be able to let go and love him back. He'd believed her feelings were right there, ready to burst free. Talk about being wrong.

She touched his arm. "I'm honored. Truly. I know this is a big deal. To be honest, some of what you said before is true. I do kind of hold back emotionally. So why push that? Why risk tying yourself down with someone who isn't exactly what you want?"

"Don't try to make this about me," he told her, feeling his temper rise. Anger might just be a mask for the pain of rejection, but right now a mask seemed like a good idea. "You're the one not willing to take a chance."

She took a step back. "It's my choice to make. Just

because you're willing to make a commitment doesn't mean I am, too. It's a question, not an obligation."

He knew that. She was right about all of it, but he couldn't help wanting to lash out and hurt her.

"You're not making a choice," he said angrily. "You're running. Reacting to something that happened fourteen years ago. You'll never be free of your loss if you don't let yourself love again. Let yourself trust and be vulnerable."

Her gaze narrowed. "Sure. Because this couldn't possibly be about anything else. After all, the amazing Carter proposed. If I'm not falling at your feet in gratitude, there must be something wrong with me."

"I didn't say that."

"You implied it. I don't want to marry you, Carter. I just don't. Think what you want, but that's my bottom line."

With that, she turned and left. The front door closed behind her.

Fifteen minutes later, he walked into the Blue Dog Bar. Someone yelled his name but before he could answer, the half-full bar erupted in applause.

"Good job," one of the cops yelled. "Not getting dead is always a good job."

Carter nodded and waved. He appreciated the support and praise for the successful raid, but right now he had other things on his mind.

"Drinks are on the house," Jenny said as he took a seat at the long counter. "Even the good stuff."

"Just a beer," he told her.

She poured and set the glass in front of him, then frowned. "What's wrong? You don't have hero face."

"I'm no hero. I did what I was supposed to do and this time the bad guys didn't win. End of story."

"You should be a little more excited than that."

Instead of answering, he pulled the jewelry box out of his pocket and passed it across to her. She opened it and gazed at the ring.

"Very nice. I'm impressed."

"She wasn't. Rachel passed."

"Ouch." Jenny closed the box. "I'm sorry."

"Is that it? Shouldn't you want to gloat? Maybe call a few other exes and have them in for a party? Carter finally got his."

Jenny untied her apron. "I'm taking a break, Jon," she yelled to the other bartender, then came around the counter and grabbed Carter's arm. When she'd guided him into the breakroom and closed the door, she turned on him.

"What are you talking about?" she asked. "What's going on? I've never wished bad things would happen to you."

"I know. Sorry. Just a knee-jerk reaction from the biggest jerk." He sank into a plastic chair and closed his eyes. "Why didn't I see it coming? Why did I think it would be okay? I'm the one who didn't believe in love or forever. I finally meet someone who makes me want to believe and now it's going to be okay? Who am I kidding?"

He hurt from the inside out. He hurt in ways he hadn't thought possible. He looked at Jenny. "Did I do this to you? Did I make you feel this crappy? Did I make you ache and bleed?"

She crouched in front of him. "It wasn't all that bad. I loved you, but not so much that I couldn't recover. I know it hurts now, but you'll get better. That old saying about time healing is true. The edges blur. Besides, aren't you jumping to conclusions? You caught Rachel off guard. Maybe she'll come around."

Not likely, he thought grimly, wishing he hadn't left his beer at the bar. This seemed as good a time as any to get drunk.

"Rachel isn't coming around. She isn't interested in being in love. It scares her." He explained how she'd lost her family and been left alone in the world.

"So her reaction isn't about you," Jenny said as she stood and pulled a plastic chair close to his. "She's doing it out of fear."

"I'd hoped she'd be motivated by something else. Something stronger than fear. I was wrong."

He'd known there was a risk, but he'd been stupid enough to think he could win. She was lost to him. He knew that and it left him empty.

"So you're just giving up?" Jenny asked.

He looked at her. "What should I do? Bully her into marrying me? Either she wants me or she doesn't."

"It's not that simple. Rachel obviously wants to be with you. She's been spending enough time with you. A case could be made that you changed the rules with no warning. Maybe you could give her a little time to catch up."

"And if she doesn't?"

"Then you're where you are now. But if you give up and walk away, there's no chance."

He leaned forward. His gut felt as if he'd taken a hit from a three-hundred-pound linebacker. "She either loves me or she doesn't. My wanting things to be different won't change that."

"You said she's dealing with her past. Is it possible she doesn't know what she feels? That she's only reacting? Give her time. Let her miss you. See what happens before you walk away."

He shrugged. "Sure." He could give Rachel all the time she needed and then some. What did it matter? He wasn't interested in being with anyone but her. Missing her, aching for her, would fill his days anyway.

Jenny smiled. "You could have a little faith in love."

"I have plenty of faith in love. It's Rachel's faith I'm questioning."

While Rachel didn't actually expect to hear from Carter, she still missed him over the next few days. She was torn between the need to see him and annoyance over what he'd done.

He could have given her a little warning. They'd gone from pretend dating to a proposal in an eighth of a second. He'd changed things so fast, she'd reacted without thinking. Without saying anything. She had a bad feeling she'd hurt him.

She wanted to tell herself that she hadn't—that Carter wasn't capable of deep emotions. Only that wasn't true. He didn't lie and he'd told her he loved her.

When she thought about him saying that, she got all gooey inside. Like she wanted to give the world a hug. But then she thought about marriage and her whole body went cold.

Marriage was out of the question. Maybe it was her past. Maybe he was right and she did keep people at arm's length. So what? It was her right. All she knew was that she wasn't interested in forever.

But she hadn't meant to reject Carter like that. He'd proposed and she'd acted badly so the next step was up to her. Even without marriage, there was still the baby to consider.

She picked up the phone, then put it down. She had no idea what to say to him. Obviously they should talk, but about what?

She reached for the phone, but this time it rang. She snatched up the receiver.

"Hello?"

"Rachel! It's Nina. I'm cooking dinner on Friday night. Just family. I feel the need to have everyone I love around my table. Six o'clock. Say you'll be here."

"I…" She opened her mouth to refuse, then hesitated. Nina was going to be her baby's grandmother and the only grandparent. Sure, the night might be awkward, but better to get that awkwardness over now. Plus, Rachel wanted an opportunity to talk to Carter. "I'd love to."

"Good. I know you have to work, so don't worry about bringing anything. I'll see you then."

"I'm looking forward to it," she said, and meant it.

* * *

She arrived a few minutes early and found that nearly everyone else was already there. Although she'd braced herself for a cool greeting and lots of questions, no one acted as if anything were different.

"You're glowing," Merry said as she hugged Rachel. "I look like a cow when I'm pregnant, but I can see you're going to be one of those beautiful expectant mothers. That means I'll have to hate you, but I'll get over it."

Rachel smiled. "I'm sure the glow will pass."

"That's just not how my luck goes. What do you want to drink?" Merry asked the question as she guided Rachel into the kitchen. Rachel chose flavored water and continued chatting as she tried to see if Carter had arrived yet. She didn't spot him and was a little surprised by the rush of disappointment she felt. Okay, sure, she'd missed him, but it wasn't a big deal. It wasn't as if she were devastated by the fact that he was no longer in her life the way he had been. She was only interested in making things right so they could be friends again.

Nina carried a large tray into the kitchen. "Here it is," she said, then stopped when she saw Rachel. "Oh, good. You're here." The older woman set the tray down. "How are you feeling? Any symptoms yet? Are you getting enough rest? You have to eat, too. Lots of good, healthy food for you and the baby."

"I'm doing well," Rachel said, still startled that everyone was being so nice. She'd come prepared to tell her side of the story, but there didn't seem to be a story to tell. Was it possible that Carter hadn't said anything? She knew he was close to his family. Wouldn't he mention that he'd proposed and she'd refused?

Apparently not, she thought a half hour later as Nina urged them to sit down to dinner. She hadn't actually seen him yet. While the women had hung out in the kitchen, the guys had been in the family room watching the end of a college football game. She'd tried to think up an excuse to casually go in, but hadn't come up with one. Funny how before the proposal, she would have simply walked back and joined him. Now, that didn't feel right.

From what she could tell, he hadn't said a word about his proposal or her rejection—which was really nice of him and probably explained the sudden rapid beating of her heart when he walked into the dining room.

He looked good. Relaxed and handsome. She took in his features, as if she'd been hungry to see them again.

He glanced at her and nodded. "Hey, Rachel. How's it going?"

She blinked. How's it going? That was it?

She looked around the room, but no one seemed to notice anything was different between them. No one had realized she and Carter weren't what they had been before. Even though she didn't know exactly what that was.

She found herself sitting across from him, and that meant she couldn't avoid looking at him. When he caught her eye, he smiled, which should have been great, but wasn't. There was something missing in that smile. It was casual, meaningless, as if she wasn't special anymore. Until just now she hadn't appreciated how much she liked being special in Carter's world.

Dinner was the usual mix of great food and fast-paced conversation. Rachel relaxed, thinking that maybe everything was going to be all right, when Carter said, "I have a couple of announcements."

She tensed. While she couldn't believe he would tell his family this way and put her on the spot, she knew she'd reacted badly. Maybe in his mind, she deserved this. She ran over a list of reasons as to why she hadn't wanted to marry him and braced herself for the public humiliation.

Nina looked at her son. "A good announcement or a bad one? I'm an old woman. Don't break my heart."

He reached down the table and patted his mother's hand. "You always were a little dramatic."

Nina smiled. "I know. It's charming."

"It is." He released her, then addressed his family. "As you all know, I passed the test to be a detective awhile ago, but I never bothered to apply for the job. I liked what I was doing. I've decided it's time for me to move on. There's an opening coming up in a few weeks and I've put in my application. I've got a good shot at it."

Nina clapped her hands and beamed. "Oh, Carter, I've longed for this. Finally you won't be shot at so much."

"Way to go," Frank said and clapped him on the back.

Everyone else congratulated him, including Rachel, although she felt a little lost. A detective? Since when? She didn't even know he'd wanted to make a change. He hadn't said anything to her.

She could see why he wouldn't have in the past few days, but what about before? He'd wanted to marry her? Shouldn't they have talked about a career shift for him?

Before she could figure out what it all meant, Carter cleared his throat. "There's something else."

Rachel felt all eyes suddenly turn in her direction. She swallowed hard. They thought he was going to say they were engaged.

Heat climbed up her cheeks. She looked at Carter, but he wasn't looking at her. Instead, he focused on his mother.

"Mama, you're an amazing woman. Truly. I'm lucky to have been your son. But it's time for me to have my own place."

"You have your own place," Shelly said. "Your own house."

Nina flicked her fingers at her daughter. "It's all right. Let your brother finish."

"I'm putting the house up for sale," he said. "I'm buying another one. It's about three miles away. Close enough for me to drop in, but far enough away so I can have my own life."

Conversation exploded.

"Did you know about this?" Merry asked Rachel. "You didn't tell me."

"I didn't know," Rachel said honestly, just as surprised as everyone else. She would never have thought Carter would want to be away from his family.

Nina looked at her son. Her eyes were bright with tears, but she blinked them away. "I understand," she told him. "You and Rachel need a chance to start your own lives together. This is a good thing." She raised her glass of wine. "To Carter and Rachel."

The rest of the family joined in. Rachel looked at Carter and found, for the first time that evening, he was watching her. Did he expect her to say something? She couldn't. Not like this.

She tried to figure out what he was thinking, but couldn't do that, either. Nothing about this felt right, she thought, uncomfortable and not sure what to do to make things better.

Dinner finally ended. While Rachel had started the evening hoping to talk to Carter, now she just wanted to get out of the house. She felt out of place, as if she were a fraud. She hated that Carter's family still treated her as if she were one of their own when she obviously wasn't anymore.

She picked up several dinner plates, intent on carrying them into the kitchen, only to stop in the short hallway between the two rooms when she heard Carter talking to his mother.

"No, no," the other woman was saying. "You were so good together."

"It's all right," he said. "We tried to make things work out, but they're not going to. Not the way everyone wanted. It's no one's fault and I don't want you grilling her. Or anyone else. Rachel didn't do anything wrong."

"But you care about her. I can see it in the way you look at her. Tell me it's not different."

Rachel held her breath.

Carter stunned her by saying, "I love her, but sometimes love isn't enough."

"It has to be," his mother told him.

"It's not this time. We'll be friends and raise a baby together."

"But I thought you changed your job for Rachel. I thought you were moving for her."

"I'm doing it because it's time for me to move on."

"You're a good man," Nina said after a moment of silence. "I'm proud of you, Carter. Your father would have been proud of you, too."

Rachel stepped back into the dining room and set the plates on the table. What was she supposed to do now?

Rachel waited until Carter said he had to leave, then excused herself and followed him to his house.

"Can we talk?" she asked when she'd caught up with him.

"Sure." He pushed open the front door, then waited for her to enter first.

She walked into the pleasant room. Everything was familiar and yet nothing seemed right. She didn't belong here anymore.

He motioned to the sofa and took one of the chairs for himself.

"What's up?" he asked.

He seemed so casual, she thought, watching him watch her. As if none of this mattered. But it had to. He hadn't proposed lightly. He wouldn't. She'd turned him down and he'd moved on—she should be happy.

She tried to figure out what to say. How to explain something she didn't understand herself. She cared about him, cared deeply, but he didn't want to know that. What did caring matter when she couldn't say she loved him?

Because that's what he would want. He'd waited a long time to find the right woman and when he found her, he was going to expect her to give with her whole heart. Could she do that? Could she give him everything she had?

The question had barely formed when her chest got tight and the need to run burned through her.

"You never said anything about changing jobs," she said instead. "I didn't know."

"I've been thinking about it for a while," he admitted. "It's a good opportunity for me. Interesting, important work and I'll be a little safer. That's good for the baby."

She nodded slowly. "You're angry with me."

His dark gaze never left her face. "Not yet. I'm working up to anger. Get back to me in a couple of weeks and I'll let you know. Right now I still feel like roadkill."

"I'm sorry."

"Why? You told the truth. You couldn't do it and you said so. That beats the last two times when you pretended you could."

She flinched. "That's a little harsh."

"Maybe. I'm not in a position to judge. I fell in love for the first time in my life and I got dumped. I'm still bleeding, Rachel. What do you want from me?"

What did she? "I'm sorry," she whispered. "I never meant to hurt you."

"Too bad, because if that had been the plan, then hey, big win for you." He stood. "If you're done, I've got things to do."

She hated that she'd done this to him. She rose to her feet and stepped close enough to touch him.

"I'm sorry," she said again as she put her hands on his upper arms. "You have to believe me."

He looked down at her. "That's the hell of it, Rachel. I do believe you."

She could see the pain in his eyes and she'd been the one to put it there. She hated that. Without thinking, she stood on tiptoe and pressed her mouth to his.

Familiar wanting rushed through her. He was warm and tempting and fifteen kinds of sexy.

This felt so right, she thought hazily as passion took over. She leaned in to him and parted her lips. But instead of responding, he stepped back.

"No, thanks," he told her. "Not my style."

"Wh-what?"

"I'm not going there with you. You've made it clear what you don't want from me, now I'm doing the same. We're just friends and I don't sleep with my friends."

But how could he deny their chemistry? They were so good together.

"You look surprised," he said, crossing his arms over his chest. "Don't be. I don't do stud-service and I'm not your pretend boyfriend anymore. I want it all, or I don't want any of it. All my life I'd blamed my troubles on women. The truth is, I created my own trouble by not being willing to step up to the plate. I'm not going to do that anymore. I'm taking responsibility and I'm taking charge. I'll be your friend, but it ends there."

She felt embarrassed and angry. His rejection cut her, yet she was aware enough to understand why he'd done it. A teeny, tiny part of her thought that maybe he was right.

"Fine," she said, doing her best to keep her voice from shaking. "We'll be friends. And parents."

"Sure."

There was something about the way he said the word. Something that really annoyed her.

"What?" she demanded. "You don't think I'm going to be a good mother."

"I have my doubts," he said, stunning her. "You're afraid to care too much. Given your past, it's understandable to me. But is the kid going to care about your issues? I think a baby is only going to know that her mother doesn't love her and that's not right."

She glared at him. Her fingers itched to throw something, to lash out. "How dare you say that to me? You don't know anything about me."

"I know a whole lot about you. I know you're letting being afraid control your life. I know you walked away from something that could have been good because it's easier than going through the fire. Sometimes fire can burn the hell out of you and you're never the same, but sometimes it just gets rid of all the dead wood and you're left with something new and clean." He shrugged. "It was your call, Rachel, and you made it. Now we both live with it."

She trembled with rage and disappointment. It was truly over. There was nothing left to say, nothing left to save. So she did what made the most sense. She left.

Chapter Fourteen

"It's not fair," Rachel said as she paced the length of the family room in Noelle's beautiful house. "He's being totally unreasonable. Now that he's figured out how he feels, I'm just supposed to fall in line. Well, excuse me if life isn't that convenient."

Crissy leaned back in the overstuffed sofa and sipped her wine. "You're right. What is it about guys? They manage to get it all together and suddenly the rest of us should pause and gasp in honor of that? So what if Carter loves you? You didn't ask him to care. You didn't pretend that he matters."

Rachel paused at the French doors and glanced at her friend. "He does matter. He's the father of my baby, so that has to count."

"Fine." Crissy shrugged. "So he gets points for mobility. Big whoop."

Rachel had a feeling Crissy was playing her a little—backing her into an emotional corner so she was forced to defend Carter. She wasn't sure how she felt about that. Carter might be really annoying, but for the most part, he was a good guy.

Noelle waddled in with a tray of appetizers. She set them on the large coffee table, then sank into the chair by the sofa. "One of you is going to have to help me up later," she said with a sigh. "I'm getting too big to maneuver on my own."

"Absolutely," Crissy said. "I'm happy to lend a hand."

For a moment Rachel wondered what Crissy thought about both her friends being pregnant. Did it bother her to know they were keeping their children? She'd mentioned her guilt at taking the easy way out before. Did she also regret what she'd lost?

"What did I miss?" Noelle asked.

"Rachel is still pissed at Carter. He's such a jerk."

"He's not a jerk," Noelle said. "Honestly, the poor man proposed. Why does he have to go to prison for that?"

"He doesn't," Rachel said as she moved to the sofa and sat down. The mini quesadillas were calling to her. She grabbed a napkin and picked up one. "I appreciate what he's trying to do. What annoys me is his assumptions about me. As if by not wanting to marry him, there must be something wrong with me."

Noelle sighed. "He's hurt. He loves you. I couldn't understand what that meant before, but now, with Dev,

I so get it. When I fell for Dev and was afraid he didn't love me back, I thought I was going to die. I couldn't imagine living through that much pain. It was horrible. Carter's hurt and he's lashing out. You have to give him a little room to deal with his pain."

"He can have all the room he wants," she grumbled. "He can have miles and miles."

"It's not that simple," Noelle said. "You're having his baby. That's going to connect you forever."

"I'm sure he's hating that." Rachel took a bite of the quesadilla.

"I still think he's being totally unreasonable," Crissy said. "Men are such a pain. Yes, he's had his great emotional revelation, but is it Rachel's fault that she doesn't love him back?"

"You can't force love," Noelle admitted. "It's just too bad you can't return his feelings. Then you could be a family."

Rachel knew her friends were being supportive and she was grateful for that, but she also felt a little judged. Crissy was trying to make a point and Noelle kept talking about Carter and what he'd done. In a perfect world, yes, she would have fallen madly in love and they could have lived happily ever after. But life wasn't perfect.

"I just can't," she said as she balled up her napkin and tossed it on the table. "I can't be what he wants me to be."

"Which is what?" Crissy asked. "What does he want from you?"

"He wants me to be…" Rachel paused. What had

Carter asked for? Except for her to love him back and marry him, she couldn't think of anything. "A person who loves him. It's just not me."

"That's okay," Noelle said soothingly. "He'll find someone else."

Rachel spun to face her. "What?"

"Someone else," her friend repeated. "Now that Carter understands that he can fall in love with someone, he's going to want to do it again. I hope this time he can find someone to love him back."

Right. Because that was the mature and responsible thing to want. But that would mean that Carter would get married. Rachel would be like all his other exes— except she would have his baby. There she'd be, invited over at holidays like Jenny and a few select others. She'd bring the baby and they'd all fuss. Especially Carter's new wife, because she wouldn't want anyone to think she minded.

Eventually he would have other children. Children who would make him forget the one he had with Rachel.

"Stupid man," she muttered. "It's all *her* fault."

"Her who?" Crissy asked.

"That woman he married. She's awful."

Crissy sipped her wine again. "Are we talking about Carter's imaginary wife? Maybe you'll like her."

Rachel didn't respond. She was busy dealing with the uncomfortable realization that she didn't want Carter for herself, but she didn't want anyone else to have him, either. And that thought made her exactly the kind of person she hated.

"I'm sorry," she said as she stood. "I can't do this tonight. I have to go."

"Are you all right?" Noelle asked as she struggled to her feet. Crissy rose and helped her up. They both followed Rachel to the front door.

"I'm fine," Rachel said, wishing it were true. "I need some time to think. I'll be okay."

They both hugged her and made her promise to call. Finally she escaped and made her way to her car. But instead of driving home, she circled through different neighborhoods until she found herself at the mall.

It was a Friday night and the place was packed, mostly with teenagers. Rachel wandered the first level, trying to interest herself in a new body lotion or maybe a soft pretzel. Instead, she found her attention shift to the kids passing by. Most of them were in groups, but she saw a few couples.

They were so intent on each other, she thought as she watched one girl melt into her boyfriend's embrace, then kiss him passionately in an alcove by the card store. She had never been like that in high school. Never that carefree or that willing to get involved. She'd held herself apart because it still hurt—every minute of every day she'd missed her family.

Someone should have taken her to counseling.

The thought was so unexpected, she stopped right there, forcing a family with two strollers to walk around her.

Counseling. Of course. She'd been twelve and she'd lost her entire family. Someone to talk to, someone who knew about grief, could have made a big difference. But no one had suggested it and she'd never thought to ask.

She started walking again, but she didn't see the stores. Instead she saw Brett, her first real boyfriend. He hadn't been surprised when she'd broken off their engagement. He admitted he'd been expecting it.

"You were never there," he said. "I hoped it would get better, but you were always somewhere else. I couldn't touch you."

She'd protested, saying they were both each other's first time. How much more touching could there be? But he hadn't meant physical contact. He'd meant something deeper and more significant.

She'd run then, because it was the right thing to do. Because it was easy and what she knew. Ironically, she was still running.

Where would she run to next? How many times would she turn away from what she wanted because she was afraid?

But the fear was so real, she thought. So big. It was her world. It haunted her and when she tried to dismiss it, it reminded her of how much she had already lost. Could she survive more?

Rachel arrived home to find Crissy waiting for her.

"I can't stand this," her friend said from her seat at the top of the stairs. "I'm here to meddle, so brace yourself."

"I'm braced," Rachel said as she opened the front door. "Come on in."

Crissy followed her into the apartment and set her

purse on the table by the door. "I know this is your decision," she said earnestly. "I've been telling myself this is your life and that you should be allowed to live it however you want."

"But?" Rachel asked, relieved to have someone to talk to.

"But you're going to make a mistake. I can feel it." Crissy walked up to her, put both hands on her shoulders and shook her gently. "What on earth is wrong with you?"

Rachel startled herself and most likely Crissy by bursting into tears. "I don't know. I'm so afraid."

Crissy led her to the sofa and sat next to her. "Oh, honey, I'm sorry. I didn't mean to make you cry. I'm sorry."

"Don't be. It's not your fault. It's me. I'm just not like other people. There's too much wrong with me."

Crissy pulled her close and rubbed her back. "Don't be silly. You're one of the most normal people I know. We all have flaws. We all deal with crap. Don't beat yourself up for being human."

Rachel wiped her face. She felt emotionally spent and broken. "He's great," she said, still fighting tears. "I know that. He's caring and honest and good and sexy. He has a terrific family and don't all those articles say to judge a man by how he treats his mother? He's terrific with her and his sisters."

She struggled for breath, then gave up and let the tears win.

"Sounds good to me," Crissy said. "If I could face one more first date, I'd go for him myself."

Rachel gave a strangled laugh. "Please don't. Then I'd have to hate you."

"We don't want that." Crissy wiped her face. "Come on. What's the real problem? It isn't how great he is, because that's all a good thing. Talk about a fabulous gene pool. So what's really wrong?"

Rachel straightened and dug down for the honest response. "I can't do it. I can't love him as much as he wants me to."

Crissy gave her a slight smile. "So much material to work with in that sentence. I'll go with the obvious one first. As much as he wants? Is that what this is about?"

Rachel closed her eyes, then opened them. "As much as I want," she whispered.

"Okay. Good. Why not?"

She stiffened. "Why not? Because what happens if I do? What happens then? He could die."

Crissy blinked. "At the risk of being a bitch, we're all going to die. It's part of living. You're born, you live, you die. There's no getting around it."

"I'm not talking about later. When he's had a full life. I'm talking about now. I've already lost everything once. I can't do that again."

Crissy nodded. "Good point. What if he doesn't?"

"What do you mean?"

"What if he doesn't die? What if he lives a long, healthy life and dies in his sleep at a hundred and three? He's what, thirty? So you will have lost seventy-three years with him on the off chance he kicks the bucket early. Not a great trade-off."

"Seventy-three years with Carter," Rachel murmured. That was her definition of heaven. "I could do that."

"Okay, so it's not the actual dying," Crissy said. "It's him dying too soon. So how much is enough? If you knew he was only going to live until he was sixty— that's thirty years with him. Would that be enough?"

Rachel knew her friend was leading her somewhere, but she couldn't figure out where. "I'd want more, but yes, I'd take thirty years."

"Would ten be enough? Would you accept ten?"

The tears threatened. "I don't know. That would hurt."

Crissy drew in a breath. "What about the baby?" she asked in a low voice. "When will you decide it's safe to love your child?"

Rachel touched her stomach. "What do you mean? I already love my child."

"Do you? How can you know how long he or she is going to live? How can you live with that fear?"

She didn't know what to say.

"I don't have any answers," Crissy told her. "But here's my newsflash. I've always wanted to fall in love, but I've never allowed myself. I never thought I was good enough. I had to keep the punishment on because of what I'd done. Thinking about you, knowing what you're going through, has caused me to question that. When is the punishment enough? When is it okay for me to be happy?"

Crissy shifted on the sofa and took one of Rachel's hands in her own. "You lost your whole family, your whole world. It was tragic. But a greater tragedy is that you survived only to become trapped in a fear so great you're afraid to live. Is this what your parents would have wanted? Would this make them happy? You go through the motions, but you don't feel any of it. I'm saying this because you're my friend and I love you. And because I'm afraid you're going to become one of those obsessive, psycho moms who make their kids live in a plastic bubble."

"I'd never do that," Rachel whispered through her tears. This was all too much. She wanted to go back to the way things were before. When she didn't have to hurt or wonder or feel.

Her breath caught. That's what it all came down to— feeling. Being willing to put it on the line.

"You think if something bad happens, you won't be able to deal with it," Crissy said softly. "My second newsflash is that you're not that twelve-year-old little girl anymore. You're a capable adult with a hell of a support system. We would all be there for you. You would never lose your home or your family. We go with you wherever you go. Trust us to be there and trust yourself to be strong."

Later, when Crissy had left, Rachel walked into her bedroom and pulled a battered wooden box out of the bottom drawer of her dresser. She sat on the floor and opened the lid.

Inside was all she had left of her parents and her baby brother. There were pictures, an old house key, their wedding rings and the earrings her mother had been wearing that fateful night. Their passports, unused except for the single stamp from their honeymoon trip to Italy. Her brother's favorite toy car.

She flipped through the pictures, smiling at barely remembered Christmas mornings, tearing up at a candid shot of her mother hugging her. Sometimes she could remember so much and at other times, everything blurred.

What would they think of her now? Would they be proud or disappointed? Her parents had always said she needed to do her best. If she'd done that, then they were happy. She didn't have to be the best in the world, just the best her.

The best her didn't live afraid all the time. The best her believed and had faith. Crissy was right—Rachel couldn't keep anyone from dying. It wasn't the death she feared, it was her inability to cope with it. Her inability to stay strong.

But she had been strong. She'd survived a devastating loss. She'd grown up and made a life and now she was a few months away from being a mother herself.

She turned to the next picture. It was of her parents. They gazed at each other with such love in their eyes. She smiled as she remembered how it felt to be around them. Surrounded by love. Nurtured, cared for, protected. Carter looked at her the same way. He made her feel safe and cared for. He…

Rachel scrambled to her feet. Was she crazy? Carter *loved* her. He was the best man she'd ever met and he loved her. Did she really think she was going to get this lucky again? Did she think she would find someone better? Crissy was right—they had a set amount of time on this earth. No one knew how long, but to waste it because it was eventually going to end seemed really stupid.

She glanced at the clock. It was nearly midnight. Too late to call. Too late to…

"Forget it," she muttered as she ran out of her bedroom, grabbed her purse and her car keys, then flew out the door. She was done waiting. She'd already waited too long.

She made the drive across town in record time, then ran up to his front door and rang the bell over and over. She didn't let herself think that he might not be home, that he might already have found someone else. She wouldn't imagine trouble. She already had a lifetime of doing that.

The door opened and there he was. Sleepy and mussed and the most gorgeous man she'd ever seen.

"Rachel? Are you okay?"

"No." She pushed past him. "I'm not. I haven't been for a long time."

She refused to believe it was too late. If he loved her, then somehow she would convince him to give her a second chance. If he didn't… No, she wasn't going there.

He closed the door and faced her. "What's wrong?"

"Everything. I'm so scared all the time. It eats at me. I was thinking earlier that I probably should have gone into some kind of therapy after I lost my parents. Maybe I still should, I don't know. But what I do know is that event changed me. I was afraid to care too much about anything. If I didn't care, then it was okay if it was taken away. You were right. Crissy was right. I guess everyone was right but me."

"Rachel, it's okay."

She wanted to go to him, to touch him and hold him and have him want her, but she remembered their last conversation. No part-time anything. First she had to convince him that this was forever.

"It's like my dancing," she said, speaking quickly, needing to get it all out as fast as possible. "I took one teacher's word. What if she'd been having a bad day? She said I couldn't make it and I believed her. I let one person's opinion define my life. I stopped trying. I took classes, but they were just for me. I went to my fall-back plan and became a teacher. I love what I do and I'm really glad I'm doing it, but I wish I tried dancing a little more."

She stopped and drew in a breath. His dark eyes didn't tell her what he was thinking, but at least he hadn't thrown her out.

"I have plants," she said. "They're safe. I really want a dog, but I've been too scared. I say it's because I live in an apartment, but I could move. I haven't bought a house. Sure it would have been tough, financially, but my parents left me some money. I have the down payment. I've been so careful not to make mistakes or get hurt that I've missed the best parts of life. The messy, unpredictable, emotionally scary parts. I nearly missed you."

She took a step closer and placed her hand on his chest. "You are the most wonderful man. You are everything I could ever want and more. I have been horrible to you and I'm deeply sorry. I know I don't deserve a second chance, but I'm asking for one. I'm willing to do whatever you say to prove myself to you. Just please, please give me another chance."

She drew in a deep breath and spoke the words that she'd been hiding from for far too long. "I love you, Carter. I love you. I want to be with you. I want to have children with you and grow old with you. I don't care how long we have. Okay, yeah, the more time the better, but even if it's just for today, I want to be with you."

She waited, studying his face, hoping for the best. One corner of his mouth turned up and he held open his arms.

She rushed into them and held him as tightly as she could. He pulled her close.

"I love you," she told him.

"I love you, too."

"I'm glad. I'm sorry I was so stupid about everything."

"You had some things to work out."

"I still do, but maybe we can work on them together." She raised her head and looked at him. "I want to be someone you're proud of. Someone you can depend on, no matter what. I want to be the best part of your day."

"You already are."

"You're the best part of mine, too."

She stood in his embrace and felt the strength of him, the love.

He pressed his lips to her cheek, then whispered, "I have something of yours."

"What?"

He jerked his head to the left. She turned and saw the velvet jewelry box sitting on the coffee table.

"Marry me, Rachel," he said.

"Yes." She kissed him. "Yes, yes. Absolutely. Say when. Today? Tomorrow? I don't need a big wedding."

"Sure you do. It's a chick thing. We'll have it all. Flowers, a cake, whatever you want."

She smiled. "I have what I want. I have you."

* * * * *

*Look for HER LAST FIRST DATE, the third book
in the POSITIVELY PREGNANT miniseries
by bestselling author Susan Mallery
On sale June 2007.
And don't miss THE SUBSTITUTE MILLIONAIRE,
the first book in Susan's new Silhouette Desire
miniseries THE MILLION DOLLAR CATCH
Coming November 2006,
wherever Silhouette Books are sold.*

Set in darkness beyond the ordinary world.
Passionate tales of life and death.
With characters' lives ruled by laws the everyday
world can't begin to imagine.

Introducing NOCTURNE, a spine-tingling
new line from Silhouette Books.

The thrills and chills begin with
UNFORGIVEN by Lindsay McKenna

Plucked from the depths of hell, former military sharp-shooter Reno Manchahi was hired by the government to kill a thief, but he had a mission of his own. Descended from a family of shape-shifters, Reno vowed to get the revenge he'd thirsted for all these years. But his mission went awry when his target turned out to be a powerful seductress, Magdalena Calen Hernandez, who risked everything to battle a potent evil. Suddenly, Reno had to transform himself into a true hero and fight the enemy that threatened them all. He had to become a Warrior for the Light….

Turn the page for a sneak preview of
UNFORGIVEN by Lindsay McKenna.
On sale September 26,
wherever books are sold.

Chapter 1

One shot...one kill.

The sixteen-pound sledgehammer came down with such fierce power that the granite boulder shattered instantly. A spray of glittering mica exploded into the air and sparkled momentarily around the man who wielded the tool as if it were a weapon. Sweat ran in rivulets down Reno Manchahi's drawn, intense face. Naked from the waist up, the hot July sun beating down on his back, he hefted the sledgehammer skyward once more. Muscles in his thick forearms leaped and biceps bulged. Even his breath was focused on the boulder. In his mind's eye, he pictured Army General Robert Hampton's fleshy, arrogant fifty-year-old features on the rock's surface. Air exploded from between his lips as he brought the avenging hammer down. The boulder pulverized beneath his funneled hatred.

One shot...one kill...

Nostrils flaring, he inhaled the dank, humid heat and drew it deep into his massive lungs. Revenge allowed Reno to endure his imprisonment at a U.S. Navy brig near San Diego, California. Drops of sweat were flung in all directions as the crack of his sledgehammer claimed a third stone victim. Mouth taut, Reno moved to the next boulder.

The other prisoners in the stone yard gave him a wide berth. They always did. They instinctively felt his simmering hatred, the palpable revenge in his cinnamon-colored eyes, was more than skin-deep.

And they whispered he was different.

Reno enjoyed being a loner for good reason. He came from a medicine family of shape-shifters. But even this secret power had not protected him—or his family. His wife, Ilona, and his three-year-old daughter, Sarah, were dead. Murdered by Army General Hampton in their former home on USMC base in Camp Pendleton, California. Bitterness thrummed through Reno as he savagely pushed the toe of his scarred leather boot against several smaller pieces of gray granite that were in his way.

The sun beat down upon Manchahi's naked shoulders, grown dark red over time, shouting his half-Apache heritage. With his straight black hair grazing his thick shoulders, copper skin and broad face with high cheekbones, everyone knew he was Indian. When he'd first arrived at the brig, some of the prisoners taunted him and called him Geronimo. Something strange happened to Reno during his fight with the name-calling prisoners. Leaning down after he'd won the scuffle, he'd snarled into each of their bloodied faces that if they were going to call him anything, they would call him *gan,* which was the Apache word for *devil.*

His attackers had been shocked by the wounds on their faces, the deep claw marks. Reno recalled doubling his fist as they'd attacked him en masse. In that split second, he'd gone into an altered state of consciousness. In times of danger, he transformed into a jaguar. A deep, growling sound had emitted from his throat as he defended himself in the three-against-one fracas. It all happened so fast that he thought he had imagined it. He'd seen his hands morph into a forearm and paw, claws extended. The slashes left on the three men's faces after the fight told him he'd begun to shapeshift. A fist made bruises and swelling; not four perfect, deep claw marks. Stunned and anxious, he hid the knowledge of what else he was from these prisoners. Reno's only defense was to make all the prisoners so damned scared of him and remain a loner.

Alone. Yeah, he was alone, all right. The steel hammer swept downward with hellish ferocity. As the granite groaned in protest, Reno shut his eyes for just a moment. Sweat dripped off his nose and square chin.

Straightening, he wiped his furrowed, wet brow and looked into the pale blue sky. What got his attention was the startling cry of a red-tailed hawk as it flew over the brig yard. Squinting, he watched the bird. Reno could make out the rust-colored tail on the hawk. As a kid growing up on the Apache reservation in Arizona, Reno knew that all animals that appeared before him were messengers.

Brother, what message do you bring me? Reno knew one had to ask in order to receive. Allowing the sledge-hammer to drop to his side, he concentrated on the hawk who wheeled in tightening circles above him.

Freedom! the hawk cried in return.

Reno shook his head, his black hair moving against his broad, thickset shoulders. *Freedom? No way, Brother. No way.* Figuring that he was making up the hawk's shrill message, Reno turned away. Back to his rocks. Back to picturing Hampton's smug face.

Freedom!

* * * * *

Look for UNFORGIVEN
by Lindsay McKenna, the spine-tingling
launch title from Silhouette Nocturne ™.
Available September 26, wherever books are sold.

**Introducing an exciting appearance
by legendary
New York Times bestselling author**

DIANA PALMER
HEARTBREAKER

He's the ultimate bachelor...
but he may have just met
the one woman to change his ways!

Join the drama in the story of a confirmed
bachelor, an amnesiac beauty and their
unexpected passionate romance.

**"Diana Palmer is a mesmerizing storyteller
who captures the essence of what
a romance should be."—*Affaire de Coeur***

**Heartbreaker *is available from Silhouette Desire*
*in September 2006.***

THE PART-TIME WIFE

by *USA TODAY* bestselling author

Maureen Child

Abby Talbot was the belle of Eastwick society;
the perfect hostess and wife. If only her
husband were more attentiive. But when
she sets out to teach him a lesson and files
for divorce, Abby quickly learns her husband's
true identity...and exposes them to scandals
and drama galore!

On sale October 2006 from Silhouette Desire!

Visit Silhouette Books at www.eHarlequin.com SDPTW1006

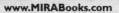

If you enjoyed what you just read,
then we've got an offer you can't resist!

Take 2 bestselling
love stories FREE!

Plus get a FREE surprise gift!

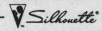

SPECIAL EDITION™

**Experience the "magic" of
falling in love at Halloween with
a new *Holiday Hearts* story!**

UNDER HIS SPELL

by *KRISTIN HARDY*

October 2006

Bad-boy ski racer J. J. Cooper can get any
woman he wants—except Lainie Trask.
Lainie's grown up with him and vows that
nothing he says or does will change her mind.
But J.J.'s got his eye on Lainie, and when
he moves into her neighborhood and into her
life, she finds herself falling under his spell....

Silhouette®

COMING NEXT MONTH

#1783 IT TAKES A FAMILY—Victoria Pade
Northbridge Nuptials
Penniless and raising an infant niece after her sister's death,
Karis Pratt's only hope was to go to Northbridge, Montana,
and find the baby's father, Luke Walker. Did this small-town
cop hold the key to renewed family ties and a bright new
future for Karis?

#1784 ROCK-A-BYE RANCHER—Judy Duarte
When rugged Clay Callaghan asked attorney Dani De La Cruz
to help bring his orphaned granddaughter back from Mexico,
Dani couldn't say no to the case…but what would she say to the
smitten cattleman's more personal proposals?

#1785 MOTHER IN TRAINING—Marie Ferrarella
Talk of the Neighborhood
When Zooey Finnegan walked out on her fiancé, the gossips
pounced. Unfazed, she went on to work wonders as nanny to
widower Jack Lever's two kids. But when she got Jack to come
out of his own emotional shell...the town *really* had something
to talk about!

#1786 UNDER HIS SPELL—Kristin Hardy
Holiday Hearts
Lainie Trask's longtime crush on J. J. Cooper hadn't amounted
to much—J.J. seemed too busy with World Cup skiing and
womanizing to notice the feisty curator. But an injury led to
big changes for J.J.—including plenty of downtime to discover
Lainie's charms….

#1787 LOVE LESSONS—Gina Wilkins
Medical researcher Dr. Catherine Travis had all the trappings
of the good life…except for someone special to share it with.
Would maintenance man and part-time college student Mike
Clancy fix what ailed the good doctor…despite the odds arrayed
against them?

#1788 NOT YOUR AVERAGE COWBOY—
Christine Wenger
When rancher Buck Porter invited famous cookbook author and
city slicker Merry Turner to help give Rattlesnake Ranch
a makeover, it was a recipe for trouble. So what was the secret
ingredient that soon made the cowboy, his young daughter and
Merry inseparable?